Som goes to Mexico!

The Adventures of Som Shekar: Book 3

Venita Jay

Table of Contents

CHAPTER TITLES 1

CHAPTER 1...2

CHAPTER 2...11

CHAPTER 3...19

CHAPTER 4...23

CHAPTER 5...28

CHAPTER 6...33

CHAPTER 7...37

CHAPTER 8...40

CHAPTER 9...45

CHAPTER 10...49

CHAPTER 11...55

CHAPTER 12...58

CHAPTER 13...65

CHAPTER 14...72

CHAPTER 15...78

CHAPTER 16...83

CHAPTER 17...91

CHAPTER 18...98

CHAPTER 19...104

CHAPTER 20...108

CHAPTER 21...114

CHAPTER 22...120

CHAPTER 23...126

CHAPTER 24...132

CHAPTER 25...135

CHAPTER 26...138

CHAPTER 27...142

CHAPTER 28..147

CHAPTER 29..153

CHAPTER 30..157

CHAPTER 31..171

CHAPTER 32..179

ABOUT THE AUTHOR..182

THE ADVENTURES OF SOM SHEKAR....................183

OTHER BOOKS BY THIS AUTHOR.........................185

Chapter Titles

Chapter 1: The Momentous Maribel Kiss!
Chapter 2: The Autumn Tempest and The Winter Storm!
Chapter 3: Som and The Wanderlust!
Chapter 4: Som goes to Mexico!
Chapter 5: Maribel's Quest!
Chapter 6: Detective Dwight Dickinson on the job!
Chapter 7: Dwight goes to Toronto!
Chapter 8: In pursuit of Som!
Chapter 9: Oh, what a tangled web we weave!
Chapter 10: To the Former Palace of Inquisition!
Chapter 11: Maribel calls Som!
Chapter 12: A long evening for Dwight!
Chapter 13: Som cooks up a storm!
Chapter 14: Strange Goings-on at The Chapultepec!
Chapter 15: Salsa Night in Mexico City!
Chapter 16: A call to Adolphus!
Chapter 17: Off to The Pyramids of The Sun and The Moon!
Chapter 18: Adolphus gets to work!
Chapter 19: Uncle Dwight, I am in Toronto!
Chapter 20: The Feathered Serpent comes through!
Chapter 21: The Feathered Serpent runs amok!
Chapter 22: Chef Som's Dips, Chips and Smoothies!
Chapter 23: Mexico, here I come!
Chapter 24: The Artist of the Year!
Chapter 25: A Big Surprise for Maribel!
Chapter 26: Alonso plans his revenge!
Chapter 27: Som's First Art Commission!
Chapter 28: Portrait Painting is not easy!
Chapter 29: Journeying to Chichen Itza!
Chapter 30: An Adventure in Chichen Itza!
Chapter 31: Onward to Uxmal!
Chapter 32: Back to Mexico City!

Chapter 1
The Momentous Maribel Kiss!

It was the Year of the Monkey! For Som Shekar, librarian extraordinaire and bibliophile, the past year had been an eventful one.

As a librarian who worked in three major libraries in Toronto, Som considered himself *blessed,* as he got to be in the company of his beloved books all day long. Working in three libraries and being in charge of the *'Rare Books Collection'* meant long workdays that stretched from dawn to dusk, leaving precious little time for anything else.

But feeling 'out of breath' as he ran to his doctor's office on that fateful afternoon of the past May had been a wake-up call for Som - Dr. Scottsdale, his favorite doctor, had assured Som that it was a simple case of allergy. But Som, who read every single medical journal in his library, wasn't entirely convinced and insisted on a cardiac exam to exclude a heart condition.

To Som's great relief, the cardiac exam was entirely normal. But that wake-up call had jolted Som into action - now, he was a man on a mission!

In his quest to shape up and lose weight, Som made a fateful resolution to 'Eat healthy and Live healthy'. Som appointed himself 'Chef' of the house and embarked on a myriad of 'healthy' diets. Sadly, Som's 'culinary delights' were entirely rejected by his family, which included his beautiful wife Priyanka and his teenage son Krish. As the sole consumer of his culinary creations, Som ended up spending a rather lonely summer, finding comfort and solace in his precious books.

In order to lose weight, Som also engaged in various forms of exercise including long walks, racing up flights of stairs, and jogging. He even went as far as trying Argentine Tango. These physical activities came to an abrupt halt, when Som was chased down the stairs by a ferocious hound named Winston, who inhabited the apartment right beside Som's. The Winston chase resulted in a twisted ankle for Som, which took its time to heal.

Winston and his master, Mrs. Moon, were dreaded by the occupants of that apartment complex in downtown Toronto. Winston terrorized not only the residents of Som's building, but also the entire neighborhood.

Winston and Mrs. Moon had a simple 'modus operandi' to get whatever they wanted. Winston invoked the imagery of 'The Hound of Baskervilles' and scared humans into submission - Mrs. Moon, for her part, felt empowered and invincible, with an unleased Winston by her side!

Numerous complaints had been launched with Mrs. Moon and the building's landlord about the unruly Winston, but they fell on deaf ears.

Mrs. Moon also greatly enjoyed gossiping about other tenants – her partner in crime was the equally unsavory Landlord Wu. Mrs. Moon and Landlord Wu would start false rumors about tenants and greatly relish the chaos that followed. The rumors started by this duo *would take on a life of their own*, causing a great deal of distress to the poor tenants.

Som had to put his exercise on hold for the entire month of July, due to that twisted ankle stemming from the Winston incident.

In mid-August of the past year, Priyanka had requested Som to accompany her to a Black-Tie event at a fancy hotel.

Priyanka was a gifted multilingual foreign language interpreter who worked with embassies and international corporations. Priyanka was frequently invited to such formal soirées in the course of her work.

With Som and Priyanka, it was clearly a case of 'Opposites attract' - no two people could be more different and yet so much in love! Priyanka was outgoing and loved parties and nightlife. Som was introverted, shunned parties, and preferred the company of his books. Priyanka was slim and sexy, always embracing the latest trends in fashion – Som, on the other hand, enjoyed his old comfy clothes and wore them till they were frayed at the seam.

When Priyanka asked Som to accompany her to this formal Black-Tie event, Som tried his utmost to get out it. Som wanted to attend a special book sale, which happened to be on that very day. As Priyanka wouldn't take no for an answer, Som struck a compromise – Som would attend his book sale first, then show up for the Gala. Priyanka warned Som about the strict dress code for this formal event and pleaded with Som not to embarrass her in front of her boss and other dignitaries by asking for his 'healthy' food choices.

But Priyanka had that strange feeling that something was about to go amiss – *a woman's instinct is never wrong!*

It was the evening of the Gala. Priyanka stood outside the hotel, patiently waiting for Som. The ever-punctual Som was late, causing Priyanka to wonder if something had happened to him. As the clock ticked on, Priyanka was getting increasingly worried.

Across from the hotel, there was a bus terminus. At 7.48 PM, the last bus arrived at this terminus and its lone occupant jumped off the bus, carrying several bundles of books wrapped in old newspaper and tied with twine.

At that very moment, Priyanka heard a cry from across the street, "Priyanka, Priyanka, I am here. I found so many wonderful bargains at the book sale. Here I am, as promised. *I was so lucky – I caught the last bus!* See, I made it. Wait for me."

The security guards, officials and guests standing outside the hotel, all saw and heard Som. For them, it was a most startling sight. It was rather unusual for guests to arrive at such a fancy event by bus. They all stared in surprise.

These curious bundles caught the eye of the police standing by the entrance of the hotel. The cops quickly whisked the bundles away to scan them for explosives and dangerous substances. Then, a special canine unit sniffed both Som and his bundles to make sure that there were no hidden drugs or explosives inside. Soon, more cops arrived, as did a crowd of curious spectators.

As the bearer of these unusual packages, Som himself was subjected to a thorough search and interrogation by the police.

This flurry of police activity, outside the venue of an important Gala attended by VIPs, caught the attention of the Press and the Paparazzi. Cameras clicked away, capturing Som and his curious bundles.

As this mystery man with the bundles had called out to Priyanka, she too became the subject of intense scrutiny by the Paparazzi.

Finally, the police cleared Som to enter the premises. But his problems were not over. Despite Priyanka's warnings about the formal nature of this Black-Tie event, Som had shown up in a casual outfit with tennis shoes. The hotel security, taking issue with this informal wardrobe and the tennis shoes, denied Som entry!

This refusal piqued the interest of the Paparazzi even further. They wondered why the cops and the hotel security had taken such an unusual interest in this strange man with the bundles. The Paparazzi followed Som's every move closely, capturing it all on film.

Poor Priyanka dragged Som to a fancy shopping mall right next to the hotel and quickly picked out a formal attire and shoes for Som.

Finally, a suitably attired Som entered the Gala with Priyanka on his arm.

Priyanka, fervently praying that Som would not further embarrass her in front of her boss and other officials, made the introductions.

Sadly, for Priyanka, it would turn out to be the strangest of evenings. It all started with the cocktails when Som asked for tomato juice with three celery sticks. Then, Som refused to touch the appetizers, nibbling away at his celery sticks – this refusal greatly aroused the curiosity of an official, who asked Som the reason for his rejection of the delicious appetizers. Som, thus embarked on a long narrative about 'healthy' food, causing Priyanka to feel extremely embarrassed.

Then, things took a really strange turn when the main course arrived. The two choices for the main course were 'Butter chicken' and '*Malai kofta*'. Som opted for the 'Butter chicken', but felt that the sauce was too creamy and too fattening. So, he carefully scraped off the sauce from each piece of chicken with his knife, then blotted it dry with a napkin! Now, Som's plate had the dry chicken off to one side, separated from a puddle of creamy sauce by a wall of lettuce.

This extraordinary maneuver caught the eye of not only everyone at Som's table, but also the main Chef of the hotel. This able Chef, who had had decades of experience behind him in five-star hotels in three continents, was in a state of shock that a guest had rejected his culinary masterpiece.

This utterly mortified Chef came running to Som and asked him the reason for this rejection.

A startled Som explained his reasons to the Chef and elaborated on his reservations about the creamy sauce, which in Som's opinion, was too rich, too creamy, and too fattening!

But Som did not stop there. He told the Chef how he, Som, would go about making the dish!

The Chef bowed and took his leave, promising Som a 'no-fat, no-sauce' chicken, as per Som's specifications.

This extraordinary exchange led to an awkward silence at the table. Priyanka was hoping that the earth would open up and swallow her.

But seated at that table was Maribel Villanueva, the wife of Alonso Villanueva, a wealthy oil baron from Mexico. Maribel also happened to be the daughter of the indomitable Don Geronimo, a powerful business magnate.

Alonso's formidable oil enterprise was well-known in Mexico, Central America and South America. Maribel enjoyed spending Alonso's immense fortune on herself and her various business ventures, including a health food conglomerate and a magazine on 'healthful living'.

The Som incident and the interesting exchange with the hotel's Chef had caught Maribel's eye. Maribel took an instant fancy to Som and fell in love with Som and his ideas about food.

Making a special toast to Som, Maribel cried, "To Som! Bravo! Bravissimo! I really admire a man who speaks his heart. Priyanka darling, I didn't know your husband was a famous Chef. Mmmm, how come you kept this under wraps? Want to keep Som all to yourself, do you? I don't really blame you. He's simply divine!"

Maribel then got herself a special coffee fortified with two shots of Irish Cream. This wonderful coffee put Maribel in a state of great euphoria. Maribel now recalled that the Press and the Paparazzi had been chasing after Som outside the hotel. A tipsy Maribel asked Priyanka if she would mind, if Maribel whisked Som off to work on a special project.

Turning to Som, Maribel declared, "Som, I leave for Colombia tomorrow, but we must get together when I get back. You must write for our new magazine. Maribel Villanueva is always looking for innovative ideas and new blood!"

Maribel then chuckled with relish, "Som, I heard you outlining your own recipe to that silly Chef. You really put him in his place! Maybe you could give us a live cooking demo sometime. That would be divine!"

The Paparazzi, who had managed to sneak in, were taking it all in and quietly capturing it all on film.

When the dinner drew to a close and it was time to say the goodbyes, Maribel had something special on her mind.

Maribel approached Som and Priyanka to say goodbye. She gave Som her business card and took his work, mobile, and home phone numbers.

A smiling Maribel now gave Priyanka a hug and a quick peck on the cheek.

Then, to the astonishment of everyone, Maribel held Som in a really tight embrace, with a long, lingering kiss on the lips!

"*Adiós amorcito! Te voy a extrañar mucho! Cuidate mucho, amorcito!* I'll call you when I get back from Colombia." cried Maribel, finally releasing Som, blowing him passionate kisses and looking at him longingly as she waved goodbye.

In her excitement, Maribel had quite simply forgotten that Priyanka, being a multilingual interpreter, was fluent in Spanish.

Maribel's words to Som had been, "Goodbye, Darling! I am going to miss you so much! Take care of yourself, my love!"

This passionate Maribel kiss was captured on film by the Paparazzi.

The Paparazzi were ecstatic. They had not expected *so much action* from this curious little man with the strange bundles. Earlier in the evening, the cops and the hotel security had exhibited an unusual interest in this man. Now, the wife of an oil baron from Mexico was kissing him passionately!

The burning question on the minds of the Paparazzi was, "Who in the world is this guy?"

Priyanka, who had struggled through this strange dinner, was stunned by this strangest of goodbyes, in front of the whole world, and in plain sight of the Paparazzi.

A startled Som extricated himself from Maribel and mumbled his goodbye. Priyanka rushed to wipe Maribel's flaming red lipstick off his lips, as the Paparazzi's cameras clicked away.

In the ensuing days, the goodhearted Priyanka forgave Som for showing up in a strange outfit and wearing tennis shoes to a Black-Tie event. As to the Maribel kiss, Priyanka decided that Maribel had likely had one too many drinks at the party.

As there were no calls to Som from Maribel immediately after the Gala, the incident was quickly forgotten.

But little did Som know that the matter of the '*Momentous Maribel Kiss*' would come back to haunt him!

The Paparazzi waited impatiently for further developments in this unusual saga of the little man with the bundles and the kooky wife of a powerful oil magnate.

There had been nothing exciting on the Som and Maribel front, from mid-August to December.

But the Paparazzi had in their possession that incriminating evidence in the form of photos and video footage from the Gala, which was worth a goldmine!

And so, the Paparazzi stuck around, biding their time and waiting for the right moment.

That moment would arrive, right after the passing of the Autumn Tempest and the Winter Storm!

Chapter 2
The Autumn Tempest and The Winter Storm!

S om had greatly looked forward to the Fall Semester when new students would set foot on the campus and into his library. Som loved mingling with the new students and sharing in their sense of optimism and hope.

But that past September had ushered in an *Autumn Tempest* in the form of a strange new boss who called himself William Williamson III - this strange man wreaked havoc in the library and threatened to do away with Som's precious books.

William Williamson III bragged about his many innovative ideas to boost library revenue by getting rid of books and renting the space for corporate events and weddings! To speed up his goal of the *'Great Book Purge'*, William Williamson III demanded from Som, the Chief Librarian, a *'Frequency List'* indicating the frequency of book usage in the library.

William Williamson III's insane ideas and hellish requests made Som physically ill – his anxiety manifested in the form of recurring nightmares in which Som kept seeing a *'Fire-breathing Dragon'* symbolizing his boss, breathing fire over his precious books and reducing them to cinders.

But there was a shining ray of hope in the midst of this extreme adversity and it came in the form of Xavier Orlando Mario Chavez-Escobar, the youngest member of Som's team and the go-to IT guy for the library.

Xavier remained unflappable amidst the chaos and laughed at William Williamson III's outlandish requests. He also came up with many a Machiavellian strategy to deal with the new boss. Xavier created unreadable excel sheets, partly in French, in lieu of the 'Frequency Report' the boss asked for, knowing fully well that William Williamson III could not read a word of French. Xavier's multi-pronged strategy was working miracles, slowly wearing the new boss down.

Then, one fine morning, a computer glitch in the transit system led to a complete subway shutdown, ushering in an unexpected sequence of events. Only three people made it to work on that eventful day, including Xavier, William Williamson III and Som. As Som had to man the Reference Library, Xavier and William Williamson III were left in charge of the Central Library.

William Williamson III had no computer skills whatsoever and was clueless about library operations. On that fateful morning, William Williamson III unleashed a cascade of extraordinary events, wreaking utter havoc in the library computer system which finally crashed, sending Som into a faint!

Xavier, once again, came to Som's rescue, by devising an ingenious strategy in the form of a night of unbridled Salsa dancing! Xavier was certain that William Williamson III would be so stiff and achy from the wild Salsa experience, that he would be forced to take time off from work.

The Salsa Night was a roaring success! Not only was William Williamson III stiff and in extreme pain as Xavier had predicted, but the plan bore fruit far beyond expectations and William Williamson III departed for England.

The computer crash and the great chaos unleased by William Williamson III, took over a week to resolve. When things were up and running normally, Som treated his library staff to a sumptuous Szechuan lunch to show his appreciation.

The fortune cookie that Som had picked up during this lunch had an intriguing prophecy, which read, "*Soon, you will have a big surprise! Your life will change forever!*"

When Som was munching on this fortune cookie and mulling over the prophecy while returning home on the subway, a mysterious lady with a rosary appeared before him and warned him of 'Bad omens and adversities' ahead.

This fortune cookie unleashed a strange chapter in Som's life, when random astrological predictions seemed to be manifesting and coming true!

The fortune cookie prophecy came true with the unexpected arrival of Som's nephew Bhim and his mother Charu – this duo turned Som's life upside down.

Charu happened to be an incredible Chef – where Charu went, the world followed. For Som, this meant unwelcome guests, who showed up in droves to savor Charu's cooking, whenever she visited Som.

Then, one evening, Som came home to an unwelcome surprise – Bhim had launched a Bollywood dance class in Som's apartment without Som's permission!

To calm down from this traumatic experience of '*Bollywood with Bhim*', Som poured himself a scotch on the rocks and gazed at the TV, which was playing an old movie. Suddenly, Som locked eyes with a strange woman on TV, who warned that '*Aliens were on their way*'!

No sooner had Som heard these haunting words than the phone rang – the mystery caller identified himself as the '*Alien who loves the desert*' and indicated that he and his wife were coming over for dinner!

Som realized with horror that the utterings of that strange woman on TV had come true, as two 'alien spirits' in the form of Som's sister Trisha and her husband Rocky, landed on Som's doorstep.

This was followed by the arrival of yet another 'alien' in the form of Rocky's mother, Sheila.

But Som was in for a pleasant surprise when he met Benito, Sheila's amore. In the benevolent Benito, Som found a 'Kindred Spirit'. Like Som, Benito was an ardent lover of books. Benito invited Som and the boys to a getaway in Northern Ontario to paint fall colors and catch a glimpse of the mighty Bay of Fundy tides in New Brunswick.

On this trip, Som had an opportunity to do some Plein air painting; this marvelous experience led Som to the realization that *he could paint and draw* - this opened up an exciting new world for Som.

Som and Benito also visited Som's father Mahesh in Venice. Mahesh had retired from a lifetime of working as a hotel manager and gone back to pursue his original love – art! Mahesh was studying art and working as an apprentice in an artist's atelier in Venice.

Mahesh advised Som to 'Let loose and enjoy life'!

Meeting his father in Venice did wonders for Som - after his return from this magical place, Som tried to stay in a positive frame of mind.

But Bhim and his Bollywood dancing really irked Som - Bhim also constantly poked fun at Som and his dancing!

An unexpected turn of events then brought Som, face to face with his collegemate, Paquito. As luck would have it, Paquito was a professional dance instructor. Paquito taught Som and Priyanka how to do the Chachachá.

Paquito was pleasantly surprised to see that Som was a pretty good dancer after all.

With this newfound skill in dancing the Chachachá, Som was happy to put Bhim in his place!

Som had a hectic December with many staff absences due to the holidays. He especially missed Xavier, who had left for Mexico to celebrate Christmas with his family.

Then, the New Year started with a big bang! It was the 'Year of the Monkey' and it ushered in many unwelcome surprises for Som.

First, Priyanka announced that she had to go to India for work. Upon hearing this, Krish and Bhim decided that they would accompany Priyanka to India.

When she heard that Priyanka, Krish and Bhim would be off traveling, Charu declared that she too would leave Toronto for a holiday in sunny Florida.

It was at this juncture that Som found himself in the throes of *a strange Winter prophecy, which warned that two apparitions from the past would come back to haunt him!*

This prophecy came true with the arrival of two unwelcome characters in Som's life - at home, it manifested in the form of Som's dreaded childhood nanny; at work, it took on the form of Som's former 'boss', Otto Schnell.

Otto Schnell arrived at the library uninvited, proclaiming that he was subbing for Som's associate Peggy, who was off on maternity leave.

With the dreaded Honghong nanny creating disaster upon disaster at home and Otto Schnell driving Som crazy at work, Som was truly at his wits' end.

But Som had one ace up his sleeve – although they had never met face to face, Honghong nanny and Otto Schnell *really hated* each other and had had violent altercations on the phone. Som knew that a clash between these two Titans was imminent and was hopeful that this '*Clash of the Titans*' would be the solution to his problems.

As Som had predicted, after another telephone confrontation of the Titans marked by vigorous dissent and name-calling, Honghong nanny drew a line in the sand, saying the words, "*Either he goes or I go!*"

These words were music to Som's ears.

When he set foot in his apartment that night, Som was horrified to find that Honghong nanny had *rearranged his entire book collection by size, shape and color!* To add insult to injury, Honghong nanny had also thrown away Som's favorite clothes, comfy shoes and organic food.

For Som, that was the last straw. He needed to get Honghong nanny out of his home immediately and booked her a long all-inclusive holiday to sunny Florida.

The next morning, with Honghong nanny gone, Som heaved a huge sigh of relief.

When Som returned to the library after Honghong nanny's departure, he encountered a most startling sight. The place was buzzing with Seniors of all shapes and sizes. There was a circus like atmosphere. Everyone seemed to be in a festive mood, as a travel agent was doing a head count and collecting travel documents.

As Som stood there frozen, he overheard the most extraordinary conversation between Otto Schnell and his buddies. Som realized that this remarkable gathering of Seniors, including the great Otto, was leaving on a Caribbean Cruise that very afternoon!

As Som wished Otto and his buddies '*Auf Wiedersehen*', he felt a great weight off of his shoulders. *The Curse was being lifted!* Som was no longer in the throes of that strange Winter prophecy.

With Honghong nanny and Otto gone, Som once again, got the bounce back in his step. He found a qualified and able replacement for Peggy in the form of his colleague, Mr. Damodaran. Som's junior, Charan Singh, became associate librarian. Now, Som had an excellent team at the helm of the library.

That evening, Som had a long chat with his father, who once again reminded Som to 'Let loose and Live it up'.

Then, in the middle of the night, Som was awakened by the ringing of the phone. The caller spoke a foreign tongue and broke into laughter.

"*Namasteji! Aap kaise ho*? Ha ha, I hear it's snowing like crazy in Toronto… too bad you can't join us! Here in Delhi, it's sunny and wonderful."

The caller turned out to be Bhim - he was joined by Krish. The boys were living it up in India.

His father's words led Som to deep reflection.

"Now, the library is well staffed. I have tons of vacation days left. Like Papa said, I am working way too hard and it's time to let go and let loose. I too shall go on vacation. Maybe, I will drop in on Priyanka and give her a big surprise or catch up with Papa in Venice. Or just maybe, I will give Xavier a big surprise in Mexico."

It was at this juncture that Som found himself at the conclusion of Book 2!

Chapter 3
Som and The Wanderlust!

Being a workaholic who loved his work, Som had quite simply *forgotten* to take vacation for the past several years. As Priyanka's work entailed a great deal of business travel, Som would hold the fort in Toronto. Now, also in charge of the prestigious '*Rare and Antique Books Collection*' at the Reference Library, Som was completely immersed in his work.

When he looked into his vacation status, Som was shocked to find out that he had accumulated *a whole year's worth of vacation* and would end up losing all of it, if he didn't act soon!

In the past, such 'unused vacation days' would be tagged on to the 'Years in Service', when it came to calculating the retirement pension – Som was horrified to learn that this policy was no longer in play. Those good old days were long gone. Now, if one did not take vacation for a really long time and failed to take any leave at all by a certain deadline, one would forfeit it all.

Som thus came to the realization that unless he acted promptly, he would be that *prize idiot who lost a year's worth of paid vacation* for no good reason!

After a snowstorm had dumped about 4 feet of snow in Toronto, the temperatures had plummeted - it was now bitterly cold, with the temperature hovering around -20•C; the frigid arctic air made things infinitely worse. This cold spell was expected to last for days. While the snow ploughs were working overtime, there was really no place to dump all this accumulated snow. The streets looked like skating rinks – for kids, it was a time to celebrate – it was fun to build a snowman and play outside.

For Som, who was no fan of this bone-chilling weather, the obvious vacation choice was a sunny destination.

"Should I join Priyanka and the boys in India or go somewhere else?" Som wondered.

Som was well aware that Priyanka had an extremely busy schedule in India – it seemed rather inopportune to land in India when Priyanka was all tied up with work. And from the last conversation he had had with Bhim and Krish, the boys had just enrolled at a local college - Som did not want to be a distraction and lure the boys away from their studies.

Som wondered about visiting his father Mahesh in Venice. But Mahesh was busy preparing for his one-man art exposition in Venice. Som decided that he should not disturb his father – besides, there were better times of the year to visit Europe than right in the middle of Winter.

Som's mother Charu was off somewhere in Florida. Som and his mother had little in common – Som loved books and his peace and quiet. Charu, in contrast, was not a fond consumer of books. She liked to live it up and go on shopping sprees. Charu also happened to be a gourmet Chef, who scoffed at Som's ideas about 'healthy diets' and laughed at Som's cooking!

After much deliberation, Som came to an important decision – he would visit Mexico City and drop in on Xavier. And Priyanka could join him there as soon as she was finished with her assignment. It had been ages since the two of them had gone anywhere - a romantic holiday in beautiful *México* would be the perfect getaway!

Som called Priyanka to give her this most incredible news, "Darling! I have a year's worth of unused vacation which I must use up immediately, or risk losing it all. So, guess what, I am off to Mexico City. And I, Som, invite you my beloved Priyanka, to join me on this romantic holiday in the Land of The Aztecs and The Maya. We shall visit the Aztec and Mayan ruins in Mexico and beyond. And best of all, it will be just you and I, taking in the beauty and majesty of this enchanting land. It will be an adventure of a lifetime! So, darling, how soon can you join me?"

Priyanka was surprised beyond belief, "What? My workaholic husband is planning to take time off from work and let loose in Mexico? And he is inviting me for a romantic holiday? Am I hallucinating? Is this for real?"

But the invitation from Som was very real and Priyanka gladly accepted, promising to join him as soon as she wrapped up her assignment in India.

Som and Priyanka agreed that the boys, who had just started their Winter semester, should focus on their studies. So, it would be a romantic getaway, exclusively for Som and Priyanka.

An excited Som got busy with his travel preparations for Mexico. He informed his associates of his plans, explaining that he would forfeit a whole year's worth of vacation if he failed to take leave immediately.

Mr. Damodaran, Charan Singh and the other library staff congratulated Som on his excellent decision.

"You deserve a great vacation, Sir. You have nothing to worry about on the library front. Charan Singh and I will hold the fort. Xavier should be back soon too. Go and have a great holiday, Sir. Give my warmest wishes to Priyanka Madam!"

cried Mr. Damodaran, who was rather old-fashioned and formal in his ways and insisted on addressing Som as 'Sir'.

"*Balle, Balle!* About time you took some vacation, Som. You don't want to be that fool who gave up a year's worth of vacation for no good reason, do you? Go for it, there is no time to waste." cried Charan Singh.

Som was touched by the warmth of his colleagues and thanked them profusely.

Now, he was ready to take off on an adventure of a lifetime.

Would Som realize his dream of a romantic holiday with Priyanka?

Chapter 4
Som goes to Mexico!

An ecstatic Som packed his bags for his sojourn to Mexico – he wasn't sure when exactly Priyanka could join him, but the mere thought of seeing her filled him with anticipation and excitement.

Priyanka herself had no clue when she could make it to Mexico, as her current assignment in India did not have set dates and might end relatively soon or drag on for a while.

But Som wasn't worried – if Priyanka could come right away, he would be the happiest man on earth. On the other hand, if Priyanka was tied up in India, Som would utilize those precious days to brush up on his rusty Spanish and devise an exciting travel itinerary for his beloved Priyanka.

Learning Spanish had been a long-time goal for Som. As Som's father Mahesh had worked as a manager of an international chain of hotels, Som had had a nomadic existence all through his childhood, moving from country to country. When Som turned seven in beautiful Singapore, his life was uprooted by the arrival of a new nanny. Som really dreaded Honghong nanny, who stayed on with Som and the family for years to come, following them around the world.

Honghong nanny made Som's life utterly miserable – she laid down strict ground rules for the young Som and banned fun childhood activities.

Som had just started learning Mandarin Chinese when Honghong nanny stepped into his life. Honghong nanny forbade the young Som from speaking any language other than English at home. *There was an ulterior motive to this directive*

– Honghong nanny spoke Mandarin and wanted to keep it exclusively for her private conversations. Som's parents Mahesh and Charu, spoke no Mandarin and Honghong nanny liked it that way. When it came to Som, Honghong nanny decided to curb his Mandarin speaking as much as possible!

Having started this policy in Singapore, Honghong nanny kept it up in other countries as well.

This meant that *Som got exposure to foreign languages only at school* and had to switch back to English at home – as a result, poor Som would learn a bit of this language and that during his country hopping all through his childhood, but have no mastery in any of these tongues.

This dictate of Honghong nanny had a lasting impact on Som – whenever he tried to speak a language other than English, there were a number of hilarious outcomes. As Som's father worked in Spain right after the Singapore stint, Som *did study Spanish* in school, but strange things would happen when Som made attempts to speak in Spanish - Som would often break into a flurry of Mandarin Chinese or come up with a curious hodgepodge of Chinese and Spanish!

On this trip to Mexico, Som hoped to improve his Spanish and impress his beloved Priyanka.

When Som asked Xavier to suggest a suitable hotel in Mexico City, Xavier would hear none of it.

"There is no way you are staying at a hotel in Mexico City – you, my dear Som, shall be an honored guest in my home."

Som thanked Xavier but insisted that he did not wish to be a bother and would hate to impose on Xavier's parents.

"Besides, Priyanka will be joining me soon and it will be nice to have our own place. Also, I want to explore new horizons in my cooking - I don't think your Mama will appreciate another Chef in the kitchen."

"My mama will definitely boot you out of her kitchen. '*Cocinar*' is Mama's favorite pastime and she will not tolerate any interference in her '*Cocina*' for sure. Hey, wait a minute, I just thought of the perfect spot for you. My Tía Thelma, who is my Mama's cousin, runs a sort of a guesthouse – she rents her upstairs to tourists and her place is quite charming. I am assuming you don't want a hoity-toity five-star hotel. Tía Thelma's upstairs flat has a room with a kitchenette, attached bathroom and balcony. Tía Thelma won't mind if you do your own cooking. She also speaks good English - I think you'll get along famously!"

Xavier continued, "Besides, my Tío Bernardo, Tía Thelma's husband, drives a cab. He is quite a character! For you, a ride in Tío Bernardo's '*mula*' will be quite an adventure. Tío Bernardo *does not care for speed limits* but he's an excellent driver. He's been driving from the age of seven. Tío Bernardo could chauffeur you around town. Yes, that will work out perfectly for you. You won't have to hop into an unknown cab; you will be safe with Tío Bernardo."

Som was very pleased with Xavier's recommendations – to have his own flat in Mexico City and Xavier's Uncle as a chauffeur would be just perfect.

When Som landed in Mexico City, Xavier welcomed him with a great big hug.

"Som, you finally made it. If anyone deserves a holiday, it's you. I'll take you to your new abode in Tía Thelma's casa first. It is in Colonia Reloj, just steps from my home. This evening, we'll have dinner at my place – Mama and Papa are eagerly waiting for you. Mama has been cooking all day in your honor."

After they left the airport, Som was in for a shock - Xavier, now on his home turf, was a muchacho of boundless energy. And it showed in his driving. Xavier seemed to whiz past a great many cars without any attention to speed limits, whistling that famous tune, '*La Adelita*'.

"Aren't we going rather fast, Xavier?" Som asked nervously.

"Don't worry amigo, you are in my hometown now. Tía Thelma is eager to meet you and I don't want to keep her waiting."

Xavier drove on as if it were the Grand Prix! At times, the turbulent driving caused Som to close his eyes and say a little prayer.

Som asked if Xavier had learned driving from his Tío Bernardo, who according to Xavier, was not fond of speed limits.

Xavier laughed and replied in the affirmative. Soon, they landed in front of a cheerful little house, painted a bright yellow, with a nice garden filled with beautiful flowers.

"Tía Thelma, here's my boss and best friend, Som. The best boss one could have. Som, Tía Thelma speaks pretty good English. I told her you studied a bit of Spanish in school as a kid and you were planning to take Spanish lessons here. Tía Thelma is ready to be your tutor."

Tía Thelma gave Som a great big hug and cried, "Welcome to my home, Somcito! Xavier tells me your beautiful *esposa* is coming too. I am very happy to have Xavier's friend and boss in my home!"

Som was overwhelmed by the warm reception, "*Tía Thelma, es mi placer conocerla.* It is a great honor and a great pleasure to meet you! Xavier is indeed my best friend and soulmate at work. You have a beautiful house and I am honored that you would receive me in your home. It is most gracious of you to offer to teach me Spanish."

"Ay, Somcito, you teach me *inglés*, I teach you *español.* Come, you must be hungry. You too, Xaviercito, I made your favorite enchiladas, mole and flan. Come on muchachos, lunch's ready."

Chapter 5
Maribel's Quest!

While Som was on top of the world in his new abode in Mexico City, Maribel Villanueva had just landed in Toronto in search of Som!

Meeting Som at the Toronto Gala that past August had been a momentous occasion for Maribel. The instant she laid her eyes upon him, Maribel was smitten with Som.

Being the wife of an oil baron and the daughter of a wealthy industrialist, Maribel lived a life of great opulence. Maribel was a very attractive woman, taking after her beautiful mother, who at one time, had been a famous model. Maribel was an only child and the sole heir to her father's enormous fortune.

As an only child of a rich father, Maribel had had a carefree existence. Maribel's interest in 'low calorie diets' and 'healthy living' came from observing her ex-model mother, who pursued the fountain of youth and went on all sorts of diets to stay slim and maintain her youthful figure.

Maribel had inherited the business savvy from her father - she took her mother's diets a step further and launched a health food conglomerate. During a promotional campaign which was simultaneously launched all over Latin America and in Miami, Maribel ran into Alonso Villanueva, the all-powerful oil magnate, whose mighty empire stretched across Mexico, Central America and South America.

Alonso was captivated by Maribel's beauty and brains - after a brief period of courtship, the two tied the knot.

Alonso Villanueva was fiercely possessive of his pretty wife and jealous of any man in her vicinity! As Maribel traveled a great deal for promoting her business, Alonso kept close tabs on her to see what she was up to.

Maribel's industrialist father had appointed bodyguards for Maribel's safety – her two faithful bodyguards, Nacho and Oscar, had been watching over Maribel since she was a child and were fiercely protective of her.

Alonso approved of Nacho and Oscar as Maribel's bodyguards. Their fatherly affection for Maribel, coupled with the fact that they were no longer young handsome men, was particularly appealing to Alonso.

Maribel was pretty in her own right, but was also buddies with a great plastic surgeon in Cancun. Over the years, Maribel had had various things tweaked and tucked, not that they needed any tweaking or tucking, but it made her feel great. Interventions by this plastic surgeon cum buddy, Dra. Zara Olifantes, also met with Alonso's approval.

When Maribel ran into Som at that August 15th gala in Toronto, she was inextricably drawn to Som - Maribel herself couldn't explain why and had even gone into it in depth with her analyst.

Som was not handsome in any traditional sense and sported a bit of a tummy, but Maribel felt that the tummy issue was easily fixable with diets or a quick tummy-tuck. Som reminded Maribel of a cuddly teddy-bear. The fact that he was also into diets and health food was another huge plus for their 'relationship'.

Granted, there was no 'relationship' between the two of them yet, except in Maribel's mind. But Maribel had one big problem – Priyanka was stunningly beautiful and it was going to be quite an uphill battle to surmount this obstacle.

Maribel also loved her husband Alonso, and had no intentions of abandoning him. Their marriage itself, was on a firm footing, but both, from time to time, would give in to their temptations, Alonso more so than Maribel.

Since that night in August, Maribel had become utterly infatuated with Som!

After she took leave of Som on the night of August 15th, Maribel underwent a number of interventions in the hope of getting one up on Priyanka and winning Som's heart. These included a nose job, surgery to take care of crow's feet, a few Botox sessions, as well as lip augmentation. When Maribel was finally satisfied with her new look, she boarded her private jet and headed for Toronto, in pursuit of her Somcito!

By sheer coincidence, this also happened to be the exact moment, when one of the Paparazzi named 'Barracuda', got impatient waiting for action in the Som-Maribel Saga and chose to send one of the 'Maribel Kiss' pics to Alonso, with a cryptic note, *"Barracuda knows all!"*

From the Toronto airport, Maribel's limo took her to each of Som's libraries where she was told that he was on vacation. No further details were forthcoming.

The limo was driven by Nacho, while Oscar accompanied her into the libraries.

Maribel had already done her homework and knew where Som lived in downtown Toronto.

As the limo pulled up in front of Som's apartment complex, Maribel ran into Mrs. Moon, who was just about to step out for a stroll.

Seeing a limo with a chauffeur and an elegantly dressed woman accompanied by a bodyguard, Mrs. Moon sensed that Maribel was someone of importance.

With a big smile, Mrs. Moon approached Maribel, "Excuse me, Madam! Are you looking for someone? May I be of any assistance?"

"Yes, indeed! I am looking for Som Shekar. Would you happen to know which apartment he lives in?"

"You mean SS? Of course, I know dear SS – that's what we call him around here. Why, he happens to live right next door to me - SS is my dear neighbor! I am Mrs. Moon. And you are?"

"I am Maribel Villanueva. I am urgently trying to locate Som on a matter of great importance. I didn't have much luck in the library. Do you know where he is?"

"Of course, Dear, Mrs. Moon knows all! But tell me, it seems to me, you are not from these parts. Am I right?"

"Oh yes, Mrs. Moon, how very clever of you. I flew in from Colombia."

"Oh my, then, you must drop by for a cup of tea. Mrs. Moon won't take no for an answer. We shall have a cup of tea and Mrs. Moon will tell you all you want to know about dear SS."

For the next two hours, Mrs. Moon spoke nonstop and shared juicy tidbits about Som, Priyanka and Krish.

Maribel was thrilled to note that this Mrs. Moon did not like Priyanka one bit.

"This woman hates Priyanka with a passion - she might make a great ally!" thought Maribel.

For Maribel, the most thrilling news was Mrs. Moon's revelation that Priyanka was off to India on a work assignment and her darling Som, was all by himself in Maribel's favorite *México!*

Maribel thanked Mrs. Moon and directed Nacho and Oscar to take her pronto to Mexico City.

An excited Mrs. Moon rushed over to bring Landlord Wu up to date.

In customary fashion, Mrs. Moon embellished the story quite a bit, "You won't believe what I just heard. First, pour me a scotch, then I'll give you the scoop. *Our SS is having an affair with a Maribel!* Can you believe it? Our quiet, boring SS is all of a sudden, a dashing Romeo. And all because that Priyanka abandoned him and left for India. I am sure their marriage is on the rocks. I wonder who Priyanka's seeing behind his back. Do you think it will be a messy divorce? This is so exciting. I can't wait to tell my friends. If you hear anything, keep me informed. Bottoms up!"

Chapter 6
Detective Dwight Dickinson on the job!

Alonso Villanueva was fuming. He looked over and over at the Maribel pic he had just received. Whoever had sent it, had attached a cryptic note, *"Barracuda knows all!"*

Alonso's mind was filled with a flurry of disconcerting thoughts and questions, "Who is this Barracuda? What does he want? When and where was this picture taken? Why is Maribel passionately kissing another man? Who is the object of her affection? Wait till I lay my hands on him."

Alonso was fiercely possessive of his Maribel. It did not matter that Alonso had a fling here and a fling there with a bevy of beauties, but Maribel in the arms of another man? No, that was unthinkable. It was simply unacceptable.

"I will find this guy. He will be mincemeat! Nobody messes with the wife of Alonso Villanueva. *Lo voy a matar!* I'll kill him!" cried Alonso in a rage.

But first, he had to locate this fiend, in order to finish him off.

For matters of this nature, Alonso used his favorite detective agency, with its headquarters in Texas. In particular, Alonso liked the head of this detective agency, a Mr. Dwight Dickinson.

Dwight Dickinson had grown up in El Paso, right across the border from Ciudad Juárez. Dwight had flunked most subjects in school, but had one thing going for him - he was gifted with languages and was fluent in Spanish.

After a string of unsuccessful career choices, Dwight had a brilliant idea one morning when he put up a big sign, on the top floor of his house.

The sign read in big bold letters, "Dwight Dickinson Detective Agency".

Dwight waited for a good two months for some action, but there was none - there were simply no clients to speak of.

Then, Dwight had another great brainstorm - he decided to put up some billboards with bilingual signs in English and Spanish! He also placed ads in Ciudad Juárez across the border in Mexico, offering his services to one and all.

The bilingual strategy worked. Work started pouring in. In no time at all, Dwight had a thriving business and more work than he could handle.

Initially, Dwight's work mainly entailed following an unfaithful spouse and documenting the infidelity with photos, audio and video, but slowly, the repertoire of his practice expanded to other types of cases as well.

Dwight hit the jackpot when he ran into Alonso Villanueva!

Dwight quickly figured out that Alonso Villanueva was an extremely jealous man when it came to his pretty wife, Maribel. Maribel, as the head of a health food conglomerate, went on lots of business trips to promote her brand - any time she interacted with another man, Alonso hit the roof and called on Dwight to tail his beloved wife.

Dwight could not understand why Alonso got himself into such a frenzy, when nothing terribly exciting was going on with Maribel. Dwight had been tailing Maribel on a number of missions and so far, he had drawn a complete blank.

For Dwight, this extreme lack of action made the job rather boring and monotonous, but the money was great and Dwight had no complaints. Besides, Alonso's never-ending jealousy guaranteed a steady stream of income for Dwight and his nephew, Adolphus Rex.

Adolphus Rex was the son of Dwight's younger sister, Eunice. Dwight had tried his best to say 'NO', when Eunice showed up with Adolphus one morning, demanding that Dwight take her son under his wing.

Dwight had resisted all he could, but Eunice had a forceful personality and always got what she wanted.

Adolphus had been an utter disaster at school – after he dropped out of school, Eunice found him a succession of odd jobs, but Adolphus managed to get fired from every job in the very first week and sometimes, even the very first day.

Having Adolphus lounging around the house was no fun, so, Eunice dumped him on her big brother Dwight.

Dwight knew Adolphus was not the brightest and could not be entrusted with complex and intricate tasks. But Adolphus was an 'okay' driver and took reasonably good pics, so Dwight kept him in his employ.

Dwight hadn't heard from Alonso in a while, but he was not worried. As long as there were men on earth, Alonso would pick some candidate to be jealous of, so it was only a matter of when, not if.

Dwight was right. His phone rang at 2 AM on that January morning. It was Alonso calling.

Alonso was hopping mad and had an urgent assignment.

The assignment was twofold.

Part One was to find out who was calling himself 'Barracuda' and blackmailing Alonso, sending him pictures of Maribel kissing another guy!

Part Two was to follow Maribel, who was off to Toronto, under the guise of a business meeting when there was none. Dwight was to find out if she was meeting the man in the picture and if that were the case, document their infidelity and bring the incriminating evidence to Alonso.

Alonso vowed to get even and deliver swift justice to this intruder in his love life.

And so, Detective Dwight Dickinson sprang into action and set off full steam on his new assignment.

Chapter 7
Dwight goes to Toronto!

Dwight Dickinson was a pudgy, heavyset man with a pencil mustache and a birthmark in the form of a port-wine stain over the right forehead. This birthmark was shaped rather like his favorite childhood mutt and for Dwight, it was a badge of honor!

Dwight wore glasses with thick lenses – without them, he was blind as a bat. As Dwight got on in years, he needed reading glasses too, so he used two sets of eyeglasses, one for distance and one for reading. Dwight could never get used to bifocals or multifocal lenses and felt dizzy and unsteady on his feet when he put them on. So, Dwight stuck to his two sets of glasses with different colored frames to tell them apart – blue for distance and red for reading.

If he had an assignment which entailed sitting under the blazing sun for hours on end, Dwight wore special prescription sunglasses. This system of these three distinct sets of glasses worked well, unless some idiot like Adolphus came along and messed it up.

Adolphus was also severely myopic like his Uncle Dwight and went to the same optician. Sometimes, the absentminded Adolphus would pick up Uncle Dwight's glasses by mistake and take off with them, leaving his uncle in the lurch.

The rather visible birthmark was somewhat problematic for Dwight when he was tailing someone and wanted to remain incognito - for the most part, he was able to successfully conceal it with a baseball cap or a wide brimmed hat, positioned strategically to cast a shadow over the birthmark. This cap or hat also covered Dwight's nearly bald head with its few remaining strands of hair. This system also worked quite successfully, unless Adolphus took off with Dwight's cap or hat, which he frequently did.

After getting this 'high-priority' assignment from Alonso, Dwight was on the first available flight to Toronto, in search of Maribel. Luckily for him, Dwight was in possession of a great clue as to Maribel's recent whereabouts, *one which was unknowingly provided by Maribel herself!*

The flighty Maribel had snapped a selfie standing in front of Som's apartment in Toronto and sent it to Alonso with the caption, "In beautiful Toronto for a business meeting... *Te amo. Besos.*"

Alonso, who had come to learn that there was no such business meeting in Toronto, promptly forwarded this crucial pic to Dwight, who used the embedded data in the photo to figure out Maribel's location.

Poor Dwight! By the time he landed in Toronto and reached Som's apartment, Maribel had already taken off for Mexico City in search of Som.

But Dwight was not one to give up so easily. He decided to look around and ask questions and ran into a great source of information in the form of Mrs. Moon.

Generally, a 'detective' would have to go to great lengths to pry some information out of an informant, but this Mrs. Moon seemed to be most eager to talk and share everything she knew.

Mrs. Moon informed Dwight that a pretty woman named Maribel had been nosing around, asking about Mrs. Moon's neighbor, Som.

Dwight quickly surmised that only a fraction of Mrs. Moon's information was likely to be accurate, but he took it all in. Like Maribel, Dwight sensed that Mrs. Moon did not like Som's wife Priyanka at all and might make a useful ally.

Dwight learned from Mrs. Moon that Som worked in three libraries in Toronto. He also learned that Som's wife, son and nephew were off to India, while Som was holidaying in Mexico City, all by himself.

Mrs. Moon also volunteered the information that the pretty Maribel, who had come in search of Som, was now headed for Mexico City to meet him there.

Although he had missed Maribel, Dwight felt that he had made tremendous progress – thanks to Mrs. Moon, he now knew the current whereabouts of this Som and where exactly Maribel was headed.

After her conversation with Dwight, an excited Mrs. Moon ran over to Landlord Wu, to update him about the latest developments in the Som Saga.

"I met a really strange man with a pencil mustache and a curious mark on his forehead. He looked rather like a gangster from the Al Capone era! He was quite tightlipped about who he was and why he was interested in SS. The plot thickens!"

Dwight, for his part, phoned in his progress report to Alonso, "It is going better than I expected, Boss. Señora Maribel is off to Mexico City to meet this Som character and this case should be wrapped up quickly. I am going to do some more snooping in the libraries this guy works in and see what else I can dig up. I think I will resolve this Som issue first, then, go after Barracuda. Call you soon, Boss. *Adiós*."

Chapter 8
In pursuit of Som!

Dwight Dickinson grabbed a cheeseburger and fries along with a large coke and jotted down the information that he had gathered so far in his little notebook. Writing things out helped Dwight to think clearly and visualize his strategy.

Dwight's notes read as follows:
Subject: Som Shekar, age 46y, person of Indian origin who has never been to India
Source: Mrs. Moon, Som's nosy neighbor, who hates Som and wife Priyanka
Reliability of source: Not great, likely invents things, but might have a morsel of truth; might make a useful ally, as she hates both Som and the wife; calls Som SS
Details about the subject from above source:
Som Shekar works in three libraries, about a 30-minute walk from his residence; very boring man who works all day; is on a strange diet to lose weight; tries to exercise for the same reason; is not friendly to dogs; has a sexy wife who is always off to parties; currently holidaying in Mexico City; wife may have abandoned him and taken off for India; could be a rocky marriage with a messy divorce in the offing; teenage son is a no-good loser

Even though Dwight did not fully trust Mrs. Moon's version of things, he had gleaned a lot of useful information. Everything Mrs. Moon had said would need to be independently corroborated, but Dwight felt positive about the case.

As to the whereabouts and the identity of this Barracuda who was blackmailing Alonso, he (or she) could be anywhere!

Dwight decided that the Som matter needed immediate attention and he would catch up with Barracuda later.

Dwight headed off to the three libraries that Som worked in.

Charan Singh happened to be at the front desk in the medical library, when Dwight wandered in and pretended to look at some medical journals. A strange man wearing a giant hat, tipped over his forehead, was not a common sight in the medical library. Charan Singh knew all the doctors who frequented the library and this strange man *did not* look like an MD.

"May I help you, Sir?"

"Oh yes, I am looking for Som Shekar, the Librarian."

"He is not here today – anything I can help you with?"

"Oh, I just wanted his help with some medical journals. Do you know where I can find him?"

"I can help you with the journals - are you looking for something in particular?"

Dwight was taken aback. He wanted to do his snooping quietly without raising eyebrows and was not eager to engage in a long conversation with a librarian.

Luckily, Dwight knew some journal names and decided to go with 'JAMA', a name he had picked up from the news. He decided he would ask for something that would be *impossible* to find, to get this nosy librarian off his back.

"Oh yes… Thank you kindly. I am looking for JAMA all the way back to Great War."

"Oh, that would be in the archival section. Which Great War are you referring to, Sir?"

"Come on man, the Big One! The World War!"

"There were two World Wars, Sir. Which one are you referring to?"

Dwight gasped. This librarian was persistent. Dwight needed a quick exit strategy, otherwise his cover would be blown.

"First World War, of course. The Big one!"

"The First World War went on for over four years from July 1914 to November 1918. Which specific issue of JAMA are you interested in?"

Dwight wanted to get away from this tenacious man ASAP. This overly knowledgeable librarian made him nervous.

"All of them! Did you say, these volumes are in the archival section? I think I might wander over there myself. Thank you kindly, sorry to have troubled you. Have yourself a great day."

Dwight quickly darted out of the medical Library and shuffled out of the building.

A puzzled Charan Singh shook his head. Earlier, an elegantly dressed woman, accompanied by a bodyguard with a scar on his cheek, had tried to pry information out of him about Som's whereabouts. Now, this strange character with a giant hat was nosing around, asking for Som and all the issues of JAMA published during World War I!

Something very strange was going on, but Charan Singh did not know what to make of it all. He did not want to call Som and alarm him by telling him of these strange occurrences, while Som was on his well-deserved holiday in Mexico.

****

After Dwight made his great escape from Charan Singh, he ordered another cheeseburger with fries and a coke. The sight of food had a calming effect on Dwight. Munching on his fries, Dwight came up with his best idea of the day.

"According to Mrs. Moon, this Som is a *really boring man* who loves books and has no other hobbies. Now, this boring man is in Mexico City. *But where in Mexico City?* Does he perhaps have a friend in Mexico City? If so, does this friend work in the library here? I must check if there are any possibly 'Mexican' names in the library directory. If there are, it will be worthwhile to check out their whereabouts in Mexico City. Could it be that somebody from the library is back in Mexico and this boring Som guy is hanging out with them? Maybe I am on a wild goose chase, but it's certainly worth a shot." thought Dwight.

The library directory was accessible to the public and in no time at all, Dwight found the name, 'Xavier Orlando Mario Chavez-Escobar'.

Of course, this Xavier could be from any number of places, so the first order of business for Dwight, was to determine if this Xavier was from Mexico.

Dwight quickly tapped into his sources and determined that this Xavier indeed lived in Mexico City, in Colonia Reloj. Dwight felt that there was a good possibility that this Som might be meeting up with this very Xavier in Mexico City.

Ordinarily, looking for Som in Mexico City would have been like looking for a 'needle in a haystack', but if Dwight's reasoning proved correct, this Xavier fellow should lead him right to Som.

An optimistic Dwight hopped on a plane to Mexico City.

Chapter 9
Oh, what a tangled web we weave!

Maribel landed in Mexico City and went straight to her bungalow. Then, she summoned her usual entourage which included Valeria the beautician, Pilar the hairstylist, Lupe the manicurist and Guillermo the masseur.

The bungalow was her father's property – it was amply staffed with a cook, two maids, a gardener and several armed guards patrolling the premises. Don Geronimo had gifted it to his beloved daughter for her use, whenever she was in Mexico City.

Maribel was in a state of heightened excitement – her Somcito was somewhere in Mexico City.

"Where could my *amorcito* be? Maybe in a bookshop somewhere? Or in a library? He could even be visiting one of the many museums in this vibrant city. Or maybe, he is in a spice market, checking out novel spices for his recipes. Gosh, the possibilities are endless. I'll keep trying his phone – maybe he has it switched off to avoid roaming charges. Oh, I can't wait to see him."

Sipping her Champagne, Maribel texted the jealous Alonso, "Darling, it's crazy busy here in Toronto. Miss you. *Besos!*"

Maribel had taken a bunch of selfies in front of several landmarks in the heart of the financial district in Toronto – her plan was to send *one pic a day* to Alonso, to convince him that she was really busy, working hard on her marketing campaign in Toronto.

Maribel thought this was a very clever plan to throw Alonso off the scent.

Maribel was in a great mood, "Vale, Pilar and Lupe are on their way. With their magic touch, I shall be transformed. Guillermo's massage will be invigorating and uplifting. With some luck, Somcito will answer his phone soon. And when he does, where should we meet?"

Vale, Pilar, Lupe and Guillermo succeeded in transforming Maribel into a radiant Goddess.

But this beautiful Goddess was left with the same problem as before. Som's phone was still switched off.

Then, Maribel had another brilliant idea. Being her Papa's pet, Maribel could count on him for anything and decided to ask her Papa for help.

"*Papito*, I need a favor. I am having trouble localizing a client in Mexico City. We are supposed to collaborate on a couple of important projects and he is writing for our magazine, but I can't seem to reach him. *Papi*, you are so good at finding people! Be a darling and find him for me, won't you?"

Don Geronimo had muchachos doing his bidding all over the world – their methods were unorthodox and often outside the confines of the law, but they guaranteed results.

Believing his daughter's story, Don Geronimo called one of his muchachos in Mexico City, who in no time at all, dug up the desired information. Don Geronimo now furnished Maribel with Som's current location in Colonia Reloj.

"*Gracias, Papito, te mando un beso.* You are the best!" cried Maribel, thanking her *Papito* and sending him a big kiss.

Maribel felt empowered. Now, she knew where her *amorcito* was hanging out. But Maribel thought it would be more romantic to have Som reveal his location to her, rather than popping up suddenly in Colonia Reloj and confronting him.

And so, Maribel kept trying Som's mobile but there was no answer.

There was a good reason for this non-response. Som was not fond of cellphones to begin with - as Maribel had correctly surmised, Som did not want to incur any unnecessary roaming charges and had switched his phone off. He only turned it on to call or text Priyanka. Also, Som wanted to disengage from phone calls, emails, texts and any form of communication from work. Tía Thelma's flat had a landline which Som could use to communicate with Xavier.

****

Meanwhile, Dwight arrived in Mexico City, hot on the trail of Som and Maribel.

Dwight first phoned Alonso to bring him up to date, "Boss, things are looking good. I tracked down a Xavier from the library who lives in Colonia Reloj. I am hopeful that if I follow this Xavier, I am bound to run into this Som. Talk to you soon, Boss."

Now, Alonso Villanueva might be jealous of any man who came near his wife, but he was a just man. Alonso's bark was work than his bite – Alonso did not believe in random violence. Also, Alonso was quite terrified of his father-in-law, the imposing Don Geronimo - Alonso had to tread very carefully when it came to Maribel and the people she associated with. There was absolutely no room for error, when it came to Maribel and her friends. If Alonso was jealous of any of

Maribel's male friends, he would do his homework utilizing Dwight's services and carefully consider the evidence. Alonso did not want to unjustly condemn an innocent man as Maribel's paramour and land in a heap of trouble with Don Geronimo.

Dwight walked into a restaurant and treated himself to a double order of enchiladas and gorditas. Dwight's brain cells worked best when he was well nourished.

Making a round of enquiries, Dwight came to know of Som's exact whereabouts in Colonia Reloj. Alonso had already furnished him with the exact location of Maribel's bungalow, so, he knew where she was hanging out. For Dwight, the pieces of the puzzle were all falling into place. All he needed to do now, was to follow this Som guy, take some pictures and videos of his amorous encounters with Maribel, and call it a day.

The phone rang. It was a livid Alonso.

"Dwight, this is most infuriating. My Maribel is sending me pictures, claiming to be in Toronto, when I know perfectly well that she's in her bungalow in Mexico City. *Mentiras!* Lies! You had better tail this Don Juan and quickly bring me the evidence. Mark my words, if he is messing with my wife, *lo voy a matar*, I am going to kill him!"

Dwight promised rapid results and turned his attention back to the football game on TV, enjoying his favorite beer, *Dos equis*.

Dwight was confident this half of the case would be wrapped up in no time - he would then go after Barracuda.

Chapter 10
To The Former Palace of Inquisition!

The following morning, as Maribel was fantasizing about Som, Dwight dove into his breakfast of fried eggs and his favorite chilaquiles - corn tortillas, cut and fried, simmered in salsa, and sprinkled with lots of cheese.

Having grown up in El Paso which bordered Ciudad Juárez, Dwight felt right at home in Mexico. He especially loved the wonderful food choices and his American buck went a long way in these parts.

It was also breakfast time at Tía Thelma's and Som was ready for his first Spanish lesson.

When Tía Thelma served her '*huevos rancheros*' consisting of fried eggs, warm tortillas, salsa and refried beans, Som decided to express himself in Spanish.

"*Ay, Tía Thelma, no me gustan los jueves. Yo prefiero ensalada y leche sin graza.*"

Everyone at the table, including Tía Thelma, Tío Bernardo, and their two little twin grandchildren, Adelita and Ivan, roared with laughter.

Som had said, "Oh, Aunt Thelma, I don't like Thursdays. I prefer salad and no-fat milk."

Som turned red. He tried again, this time adding, "*Yo no como jueves.*"

The laughter got louder still.

What Som had said was, "I don't eat Thursdays."

Poor Som - he had mistakenly said '*jueves*' (Thursday), when he meant to say '*huevos*' (eggs).

The six-year-old twins, Adelita and Ivan, made up a little song about 'Eating Thursdays', using Som's own words.

Som did not mind. This was a wonderful family and it was all in good fun.

Tía Thelma's '*huevos rancheros*' looked extremely inviting. Finally, Som gave in to the temptation and tried her heavenly creation.

It was utterly delicious, leading Som to ask for seconds and declare, "*Gracias, hen haochi!*"

As everyone stared in surprise, Som quickly realized his error – while trying to say, 'Thank you, it's very tasty!', Som had come up with some interesting vocabulary, that was part Spanish and part Chinese.

Som apologized for this mix-up and explained to a puzzled Tía Thelma that when he attempted to speak foreign languages, he had a tendency to mix them up and make up unique vocabulary.

Som's Spanish lesson continued on all through breakfast, with many sidesplitting moments.

****

Som had reserved that entire day for a most special museum – this 'Museum of Mexican Medicine' was housed in the former Palace of Inquisition.

During his college days, Som used to attend 'History of Medicine' lectures by one of the professors on campus. His father Mahesh had gifted to Som, two wonderful treatises on the 'History of Medicine' in the Western World. Mahesh had also gifted to Som a biography of Sushruta, the renowned Indian surgeon from antiquity. Sushruta's plastic surgery to reconstruct the nose was world renowned - Sushruta performed this reparative surgery on those poor subjects whose noses had been lopped off as punishment.

Studying these 'history of medicine' texts had created a great longing in Som for the pursuit of medicine. But somehow or the other, he did not end up studying medicine, a decision he would regret all his life. Som made up for this shortcoming by poring over the medical texts and journals in his medical library.

After breakfast, Som hopped into Tío Bernardo's cab, which whizzed past traffic at breakneck speed, towards the Museum of Mexican Medicine.

Som gasped. So far, he had been in a car with two Mexicans – Xavier and Tío Bernardo. Both had identical driving styles!

"Could this be a national trend? I think not, I think this love of excessive speed must be a family trait, unique to this particular family." Som decided.

Tío Bernardo dropped Som off in front of this grand edifice.

The Museum of Mexican Medicine was located in the heart of Plaza Santo Domingo, only minutes from the Zócalo, with its famous Constitution Square.

Most tourists would have chosen to start with the Zócalo, but not Som - his heart was set on seeing medical curios and learning about the evolution of medical milestones.

Som had looked up the remarkable history of this edifice, which was the former Palace of Inquisition, constructed by master architect, Pedro de Arrieta.

Som stood in silence at its entrance, reflecting on its turbulent history during the Inquisition.

In 1854, this palace became the home of the school of Medicine. Until then, the medical school, which was founded in 1833, had been wandering from site to site without a home. In 1933, further modifications commemorated the Centenary of the establishment of this fine medical school.

Som stood on the open patio and turned around to get a 360-degree view of this grand edifice – as he turned, he noticed a rather curious man, who appeared to be walking in circles around Som!

This heavyset man had a pencil mustache and thick glasses and wore a giant sombrero tipped over the forehead, in an attempt to cover up what seemed to be a curiously shaped birthmark. As their eyes met, the man gasped, smiled, then waved.

"Must be a friendly tourist. Was he taking pictures of me? No, I must be imagining things. Why would he do that? He must be photographing this grand palace." thought Som.

This stranger of course, was none other than Dwight Dickinson, who had managed to locate Tía Thelma's house with Som in it. With his telephoto lens, Dwight had captured great shots of Som and Tía Thelma's family at breakfast. Tía

Thelma's mouthwatering '*huevos rancheros*' looked utterly divine - Dwight was dying for a bite and almost tempted to enter Tía Thelma's house under some pretext, but had to control his impulses.

Dwight had then followed Som to this former 'Palace of Inquisition'. He was indeed busy photographing Som, rather than the edifice.

The museum had a remarkable collection of relics that traced the story of Mexican medicine, from its early origins all the way up to the 20th Century. There were many medical curios, including dissected anatomical specimens and wax figures.

Dwight of course, had expected Som to finish looking at these specimens in about an hour. But to Dwight's great surprise, Som was extremely thorough, scrutinizing each and every item in the museum.

Dwight, for his part, enjoyed looking at the scary medical specimens, then, wanted to call it a day. But not Som - Som seemed to be particularly fascinated with a collection of medicinal plants and herbs and was taking copious notes.

By mid-day, Dwight was hit with terrible hunger pangs.

"Is this guy for real? What's with this fixation on plants and herbs?" Dwight wondered.

For Dwight, it was also proving to be challenging to remain incognito, while following Som's trail in the cramped corners of the museum.

Som found it somewhat curious that this pudgy man with the birthmark and sombrero, *seemed to like everything Som liked and saw everything Som saw!*

Then, Som froze in front of a desk which belonged to Santiago Ramón y Cajal, the renowned Nobel Prize winner, who had defined the 'microscopic structure' of the nervous system.

Dwight could not understand what the big deal was about this desk. He wondered if Som was okay in the head for his undue enthusiasm for a mere desk!

Finally, the section on medical and surgical instruments seemed to excite Som tremendously.

By now, Dwight's tummy was growling with hunger.

To Dwight's horror, Som remained inside this building, admiring all of its collections, right up until closing time.

In the course of his thorough study of the medical artifacts in the museum, Som bumped into Dwight a bunch of times, but chalked it up to coincidence.

Finally, when the museum closed its doors, Som stepped out, took out his cellphone and placed a call to Tío Bernardo.

An excited Dwight followed in hot pursuit and got the license plate number of Tío Bernardo's cab and more pics of Som and Tío Bernardo.

At this point, an exhausted Dwight decided to call it a day.

"I know where you live, Som. I also know what you look like. The game is on, my friend."

As Som excitedly recounted his adventures of the day to Tío Bernardo, Dwight hit the nearest bar and made a call to Alonso.

Chapter 11
Maribel calls Som!

Tío Bernardo dropped Som off at the house and took off again for a quick spin.

Som was dying to call Priyanka and tell her all about his exciting day, but Delhi was +11.5 hours ahead compared to Mexico City – not wanting to wake Priyanka up, Som decided to text her.

Being one of those rare people who used *complete sentences with proper grammar and punctuation* even while texting, Som's text took a long while to compose!

At this very moment, Maribel, who had been trying desperately to call Som all day, got through.

"Hello! *Bueno! Quién habla?* Who is calling, please?" asked Som.

"*Amor mío! Soy yo.* It is me, my Love. Oh, how I have longed for this moment. It's really you – you are really here! How I have missed you, my darling!"

"Excuse me! Hello, who's there? I think the lines are crossed. Who is this please?"

"Somcito, you Big Kidder, you! Don't you remember me? You promised to cook for me."

"WHAT? Madam, whoever you are, I am not whoever you think I am. I am sure we are having a bad connection and the lines are crossed."

"Ah so, you want to play hard to get. Well, in that case, you are Som Shekar, Chef Extraordinaire and I am Maribel Villanueva of the health food conglomerate. You promised to write for my magazine and do cooking demos for me. I went looking for you in Toronto, but you came to my favorite Mexico City, which makes it all the more wonderful. I want you to make me your 'no-fat, no-sauce chicken' that you spoke of to that silly Chef, last August in Toronto!"

Som's jaw dropped. The events of that strange August night were coming back to him.

"Hello, are you there? Don't leave me hanging, *amorcito*. Now, when do we meet to discuss your writing and your demo? I have an idea - I will organize a lunch for the Press tomorrow in my garden and you can give us your demo. I leave the lunch menu entirely up to you, but I definitely want that 'no-fat, no-sauce chicken' of yours. I will also be inviting my friends. But wait, we need a nice outfit for you. What size are you? Oh well, never mind, I'll figure it out. After this lunch, we can go over the ideas for the magazine. I am so excited, my Love. Now, be a darling and don't shut your phone off. Is there a local phone in the place you are staying at? Please give me that number. But *amor*, tell you what, why don't I come right over? *En dónde estás?* Where exactly are you?"

"Hello Maribel! How are you? I am in Colonia Reloj in Tía Thelma's house. Why don't we meet tomorrow and discuss the articles for the magazine? I would like some time to organize my thoughts."

"Nonsense! I am coming right over. After a few tequila shots, you will be energized and your thoughts will be well organized. You mentioned Tía Thelma – I'd like to have a word with her. I want to get the directions to her place. I am so excited. We are finally going to meet again!"

A stunned Som passed the phone over to Tía Thelma.

As Tía Thelma gave directions to Maribel, Som stood there speechless. He could hardly deny that it was exciting and exhilarating to be asked to write for a health food magazine and do a cooking demo in front of the Press. But why this rush? He would have preferred to ease into it.

Tía Thelma gave her landline and mobile number to Maribel. When the conversation ended, Tía Thelma could hardly contain her excitement, "Señorita Maribel, the daughter of the mighty Don Geronimo and the wife of the great Alonso Villanueva, is coming to my house. *Ay dios mío*, I wish I had had more notice, I would have fixed the house up. Somcito, Señorita Maribel wants you to write for her magazine and cook a special lunch tomorrow for the Press. *Ay* Somcito, I didn't know you were such a 'sensation' – I now have a famous Star and Celebrity under my own roof. Señorita Maribel should be here any moment. I better let Bernardito know."

Chapter 12
A long evening for Dwight!

As Dwight was enjoying his second cerveza in a bar close to the Museum of Mexican Medicine, Tío Bernardo wandered into that very same bar with his buddy, Raul.

Tío Bernardo and his buddy sat not far from Dwight and ordered their favorite libations. As the pair got into an animated conversation, an utterly delighted Dwight took it all in.

At this precise moment, Tía Thelma happened to call her beloved Bernardito.

Tío Bernardo was somewhat hard of hearing and found it easier to put the speaker on, while using his cellphone.

Dwight was ecstatic. Now, he did not have to strain hard to eavesdrop – the man had put the speaker on, for the whole world to hear what his wife had to say.

"Bernardito, get back home right away. Bring some good bottles of wine and Champagne. We have a VIP guest coming over. It is such a great honor. Señorita Maribel, the daughter of the honorable Don Geronimo and the wife of the esteemed Alonso Villanueva, is on her way to our humble home. She is coming to see our Somcito. It seems our Somcito is a Celebrity Chef and a famous writer. He is going to write for Señorita Maribel's magazine. Señorita Maribel has invited him to cook lunch at her bungalow tomorrow - we are invited too, Bernardito. *Imagínate! Tu y yo en la casa de la Señorita Maribel!* You and I will be in Señorita Maribel's mansion tomorrow, while the TV cameras are rolling. Hurry up

Bernardito, pick up the best wine and Champagne. And the best cheese, olives and grapes, and lots of flowers!"

Dwight sat up with a jolt. He had hoped to have a relaxed evening enjoying his cervezas, but this was HUGE NEWS! Maribel was going to meet her Som in Tía Thelma's house.

The Boss would definitely want pictures of this encounter - all Dwight had to do was hide himself in Tía Thelma's garden, by perching on the avocado tree.

Dwight had spotted this avocado tree that very morning, as he was capturing shots of Som with his telephoto lens. Dwight felt that this tree would be an easy one to scale and its foliage would offer adequate cover - with all the excitement indoors, no one was likely to spot Dwight, up there on a tree. The bougainvillea bush in front of the tree would offer an additional layer of concealment.

Dwight ordered a quick tequila shot for the road. After a strange day of tailing Som and staring at curious medical specimens, the evening was shaping up to be an interesting one!

Tío Bernardo told his buddy Raul about his VIP guest. Señorita Maribel, the daughter of the great Don Geronimo and the wife of the mega-rich Alonso Villanueva was going to grace his home with her presence. When Raul expressed his desire to tag along, Tío Bernardo cleverly dissuaded him by suggesting that Señorita Maribel would be discussing articles for her magazine and the subject would be too boring for Raul.

Tío Bernardo did not mind having Raul for a drinking buddy, but this evening was all too important. Señorita Maribel was no less than royalty and Tío Bernardo did not want any distractions during this memorable encounter.

Tío Bernardo ticked off all the items on Tía Thelma's list and headed home. He then put on his best suit and cologne; Tía Thelma for her part, fixed her hair and wore her best dress, then, got her grandkids ready for this great event.

****

Meanwhile, Som desperately tried to reach Priyanka to discuss this unexpected turn of events. *Maribel Villanueva had surfaced again*, after all these months, and was inviting Som to cook for her guests and the Press.

As much of the world shunned and mocked Som's cooking, this special invitation was something Som could hardly turn down. And Maribel was asking Som for his special 'no-fat, no-sauce chicken', no less.

Priyanka had attributed the famous 'Maribel Kiss' to Maribel having one too many cocktails at the Toronto Gala. Som chalked up Maribel's vocabulary choices such as '*amorcito*' and '*amor mío*' to her being a warm-blooded '*Latina*' and did not attach further importance to them.

"Priyanka is not answering my calls and texts. Where could she be? I would really feel a whole lot better running this by her, but she is not responding. Now, this invitation sounds harmless enough – Maribel wants me to write for her magazine and do a cooking demo tomorrow. The Press will be there. When will I get such a great opportunity? Tía Thelma and Tío Bernardo are also coming along, so it is not like I am going on a clandestine date. Maribel's guests and the Press will be waiting with anticipation for my delicious 'no-fat, no-sauce chicken' – how can I disappoint them and say no?" Som muttered to himself.

After trying for a good thirty minutes to reach Priyanka, Som could wait no longer and decided to go ahead. As Som had packed only two pairs of jeans and two T-shirts for his Mexico trip, his choice of wardrobe was rather simple and straightforward.

****

While everyone was getting ready indoors, Dwight managed to scale Tía Thelma's compound and find a comfortable spot on the avocado tree.

Tía Thelma's garden was aglow in the bright moonlight; Dwight set up his equipment and geared up for a night of action.

At 9 PM, a chauffeured limo arrived and Maribel entered Tía Thelma's house, accompanied by her stern-faced bodyguard, Oscar, who came armed with a rifle. Oscar had a visible scar on his left cheek, extending from the corner of his mouth to his left eye. Anytime anyone advanced too close to Maribel or made an abrupt move, Oscar took a menacing step forward.

Tía Thelma and Tío Bernardo extended a warm welcome to their distinguished visitor, who acknowledged them, then, quickly turned her attention to the object of her affection, Som!

With Oscar standing by her side like a formidable dragon and interposing himself between Maribel and everyone else, Maribel could not hug and kiss Som like she really wanted to and had to settle for a more subdued handshake.

Dwight, who was capturing all the action on his camera from his vantage point, felt a little let down.

"What? I am sitting here on an avocado tree in this garden, videotaping this strange evening and all I get is a boring handshake? What's wrong with this guy? He seems to love gory medical specimens and spends all day admiring them in the strangest of museums. Come evening, he dresses in a comical outfit with old jeans and an ugly T-shirt and nervously shakes the hand of the Iron Lady, Maribel Villanueva. It looks more like a meeting of '*El ratón y La leona*' – the Mouse and the Lioness! I hope I get something more exciting than this, otherwise, the Boss is not going to believe me." Dwight muttered to himself.

****

Poor Dwight! At that moment, a bird flew over and settled on his almost bald head which was not protected by the sombrero. The bird began to pluck on the few remaining hairs on Dwight's head, causing him to flinch with pain and let out a cry. Dwight desperately tried to get rid of this unwelcome intruder who wouldn't let go - in the ensuing tussle, the branch Dwight was perched on broke and Dwight fell off the avocado tree.

This commotion in the garden attracted the attention of the ever-watchful Oscar, who came running out with his gun drawn! Luckily for Dwight, the bougainvillea bush in front of the avocado tree provided adequate cover and Oscar did not notice him. Spotting a bird fluttering about, Oscar decided that the noise in the garden was just a bird flying about and returned inside.

Dwight heaved an enormous sigh of relief. He wanted to bolt from that garden immediately and call it a day, but Maribel's limo was parked right outside the house and Dwight definitely did not want to attract the chauffeur's attention. Dwight was sure Maribel's chauffeur would be heavily armed too.

Although Dwight was a proud Texan, he did not enjoy the sight of firearms, much less staring down the barrel of one pointed in his direction. Oscar and his rifle looked utterly menacing and Dwight wanted to take absolutely no chances.

So, poor Dwight had to lie absolutely still on the wet grass, without making the slightest sound, for the rest of the evening.

Although Dwight could not see what was going on inside, he could hear every word clearly - he recorded all of it.

****

Inside the house, Champagne was flowing. Maribel asked Som what he had been up to since the last time she saw him. Som gave her a brief summary of the goings on in the library and in his life. He told Maribel about his newfound love of art.

As Som was telling Maribel about his adventures with Plein Air painting, a brilliant idea occurred to him.

"Maribel, as I have taken up art, I have been experimenting with various art forms. I am thinking of doing still-life paintings of vegetables, then, cook them and serve them to my audience, the idea being, 'First paint it, before you eat it!' That will make a nice visual for the articles, don't you think?"

"Yes, yes, what a fantastic idea! We'll call it, 'If you paint it, you get to eat it!' Say, can you do a little art demo tomorrow, before you cook your masterpiece? That would be awesome."

"Yes, I think that is quite doable. Rather than paint the lifeless chicken, I will paint a tomato, onion and a zucchini, then, make a soup out of them. That of course, will be in addition to my 'no-fat, no-sauce chicken'. I think that should work out quite nicely."

Maribel raised her glass in a toast, "Bravo! I think this is an utterly fabulous idea. *Salud!*"

As everyone raised their glasses to join Maribel in a toast, Maribel darted forward with an inch tape and took measurements of Som's chest, waist, hips, shoulder, arm span, and arm length. She explained to the startled Som that the wardrobe for the following day's event had to be perfect. Then, Maribel took the necessary measurements for the trousers. Tía Thelma rushed over to help, while Tío Bernardo jotted the measurements down, nodding in approval.

Poor Dwight, who was lying prostrate on the ground and unable to move, missed this sartorial segment of 'Measuring Som' in its entirety.

Dwight was hoping this strange night would end soon and he would get his freedom – it was mighty uncomfortable to lie still on the wet ground, frozen in the same position for so long.

That freedom came shortly after midnight, when Maribel finally took leave of Som, promising to send the limo the following morning for Som, Tía Thelma, Tío Bernardo and the twins.

Chapter 13
Som cooks up a storm!

For Dwight, it had been the strangest day of them all. Trying to keep up with this 'purported lover' of Maribel had been an utterly exhausting experience. In pursuit of this alleged Romeo, Dwight had been up early in the morning, watching Tía Thelma's house from afar, capturing photos of Som munching her delicious *huevos rancheros*. Then, poor Dwight was trapped in a weird museum, taking countless photos of Som staring at curious medical specimens.

The evening had taken an even stranger turn, when Dwight learned that Maribel would be visiting Som at Tía Thelma's house. To document this encounter between Maribel and Som, Dwight had found himself the perfect hiding spot in the garden. He had gone as far as capturing the handshake between the couple - at that point, a tenacious avian had rudely disrupted Dwight's masterplan. The tussle with this avian had resulted in Dwight falling off the avocado tree and attracting the attention of Maribel's armed bodyguard Oscar, forcing Dwight to lay absolutely still on the wet grass, until Maribel and company had finally departed.

Although he was unable take more photos after that awkward handshake between Som and Maribel, Dwight could hear their conversation clearly and had captured the entire audio.

The events of the evening left Dwight shaking his head, "I don't believe this guy! He spends the whole day staring at medical curios. Then, he puts on an old pair of jeans and a faded T-shirt and greets Señorita Maribel with a tepid handshake and goes on about how his new love of art and *offers to paint an assortment of vegetables at her party.* The guy is completely loco!"

After ascertaining that Maribel and her armed bodyguards had left in the limo, Dwight stayed put for another half an hour until everyone at Tía Thelma's had stepped indoors.

Dwight finally got his freedom at 12.30 AM. He made good his escape from Tía Thelma's compound and began contemplating his next move. Maribel had promised to send the limo by 8 AM. It would be easy enough to follow the limo and get to Maribel's bungalow, but the place would be teeming with armed guards. Dwight had to somehow find his way in, and once inside, he would need unrestricted access to Som and Maribel, to take the pictures that Alonso wanted.

Next morning, Dwight treated himself to a double order of chilaquiles and huevos rancheros plus a big pot of coffee. Once again, this enormous breakfast stimulated Dwight's brain cells and helped him to come up with a good strategy.

"I shall say I am a reporter representing the "*Eat more and Eat well Society*" of El Paso and am covering various 'health-food related events' in the US and Mexico. It is vague enough to avoid scrutiny and I will carry some phony press credentials, in case Oscar ambles over to me with his gun in hand. But as I bumped into Som a bunch of times at the museum, I will need a disguise. I think I will wear a blond wig and a goatee, tie a bandana to cover the birthmark, and put on my dark glasses. Som, who so far looks and sounds like a complete idiot, is unlikely to recognize me in this getup."

Dwight set his plan into motion.

Maribel's limo came by Tía Thelma's house at 8 AM – a few minutes later, Som emerged, wearing the spiffy new outfit chosen by Maribel for the occasion. There was great excitement in the air as Tía Thelma, Tío Bernardo and the twins, Adelita and Ivan, all hopped into the limo.

Dwight, in his 'reporter' disguise, tailed them at a safe distance and flashed his phony press credentials to gain access to Maribel's bungalow.

****

The hour had come. Maribel introduced Som to the guests and the Press, "Friends, today, you are in for a rare treat. Today's theme will be a sublime mélange of art and food! When I heard our honored guest, Chef Som, telling a seasoned Chef in Toronto how to cook chicken, I knew we would be having him over to share his culinary delights with us. Not only will Chef Som delight us with his cuisine, but he will begin with a bit of art, the idea being, '*If you paint it, you get to eat it!*' So, please give a warm welcome to our Artist and Chef Extraordinaire, Chef Som!"

A big round of applause followed as Som started his still-life painting of a tomato, zucchini and onion. The Press watched in awe, as Som began to capture a pretty good likeness on canvas.

Dwight, who was carrying a heavy camera and capturing it all on film, could hardly believe his eyes.

"This guy is utterly mad. I am following a crazy loco around Mexico City - he is sitting here in Maribel Villanueva's mansion, surrounded by a gazillion armed guards, painting vegetables. Don Alonso is going to think I am pulling his leg when I show him this clip."

Tía Thelma watched Som painting the still-life for a bit and began conversing with Maribel. Maribel took an instant liking to Tía Thelma.

"Tía Thelma, would you mind being Som's assistant today? Could you give him a helping hand? It would mean so much to me."

"Of course, it will be my great pleasure, Señorita Maribel."

Not to be outdone, Tío Bernardo offered to help with the bar and serving the drinks, "Señorita Maribel, I used to be a bartender on a cruise ship. With these many guests, I think we could really use another bartender. Why don't I set up another bar by the pool? I could be the bartender there, by the *piscina*. It would be my greatest honor to serve you!"

Maribel was overjoyed at this warm gesture by the couple and accepted.

After some two hours, Som's still-life painting finally got finished amidst a roaring applause. Som now dismantled his still-life display and used those very vegetables for his soup. Then, he got started with his ''No-fat, No-sauce Chicken', with Tía Thelma as his able assistant.

Cameras clicked away capturing Chef Som in action.

Dwight was amongst the many photographers filming it all. Dwight was in utter disbelief, "Don Alonso is not going to believe me. I am taking shots of a guy painting zucchini and cooking chicken. This is the weirdest assignment of my life!"

Meanwhile, Tío Bernardo's 'Bar by the Pool' saw lots of action. Tío Bernardo was exceptionally generous with his spirits and *the alcohol content in his cocktails was amped up several-fold!* As the friendly bartender, Tío Bernardo got a taste of some of his super cocktails himself.

As Som was immersed in creating his chicken dish, Tía Thelma helped with the salad and the soup. She also made guacamole and spicy *salsa verde* and *salsa roja* (spicy green and red sauce) for the nacho chips.

****

A couple of hours later, Som was finished with his 'Chicken à la Som'. Cameras clicked away as Maribel and the guests broke into a round of applause. As the Press had many questions for Som, Tía Thelma offered to carve up the chicken and serve it to the guests.

Tía Thelma tasted Som's chicken and thought it was far too bland.

"Poor boy, all this attention and so many cameras must have distracted my Somcito. *This chicken is too insipid and needs something!* A touch of my *salsa verde* and *salsa roja* and some crema should do it. I won't trouble the poor boy, he's busy with reporters – I will just go ahead and fix it."

So, unbeknownst to Som, his 'Chicken à la Som', now had a touch of Tía Thelma's spicy red sauce, green sauce and crema.

Tía Thelma's additions soaked into Som's chicken, enhancing it greatly.

Now, the twins, Adelita and Ivan, were running around, utterly bored. There were no other kids to play with in this party, so they made their way to the pool. Tío Bernardo gave them a yummy mix of sweet mango juice and pineapple juice.

As Tío Bernardo was using overly generous amounts of spirits to liven up his cocktails, he soon ran out of vodka, vermouth, bourbon and tequila. He asked the twins to bring him a couple of bottles of each from inside the house.

The twins happily obliged, but while returning with the bottles, Ivan had a brilliant idea!

Seeing how happy people became when their *abuelito* poured a good shot of vodka, vermouth, bourbon and tequila into his cocktails, the observant Ivan said to Adelita, "Look how happy people become when they drink *abuelito's* cocktails. It must be the stuff in these bottles that's making everyone so happy. How about we add some of it into the chicken that *abuelita* is serving? *Let's make abuelita's chicken happy too!*"

Adelita wholeheartedly agreed with Ivan.

The twins now asked Tía Thelma if they could help with serving the chicken.

Tía Thelma was overjoyed that her adorable twins wanted to help.

So, the carved pieces of 'Chicken à la Som' on each plate, now got a good dousing of vodka, vermouth, bourbon and tequila courtesy of the twins, who went on to serve this '*Happy Chicken*' to all the guests!

Finally, it was time to taste the culinary masterpiece of the great Chef Som.

The interventions by Tía Thelma and the twins had made 'Chicken à la Som' utterly delicious.

The guests and the Press raved at this divine creation.

"Bravo!"

"Bravissimo! This is to die for!"

A hungry Dwight took one bite and had to admit that Som was an outstanding Chef.

Maribel, her happy guests and the inebriated Press, all congratulated Som on his exceptional chicken.

Maribel was ecstatic – Chef Som was a resounding hit!

Maribel decided that the discussions about the magazine articles could wait for another day. She wanted to take Som to 'The Chapultepec Palace' and show him some sights of the marvelous Mexico City.

Maribel thanked Tío Bernardo and Tío Thelma for their help and showered them with gifts – the happy couple and the twins left for home in one of Maribel's limos.

Now, Maribel made a little speech to the guests and the Press, thanking them for attending this special event and told them to look out for the next issue of her health food magazine, "*Salud, Vida y Mucho Más!*" (Health, Life and Much More!) for the upcoming series by Chef Som.

Chapter 14
Strange Goings-on at The Chapultepec!

When Dwight heard that Maribel and Som were now headed to The Chapultepec, his jaw dropped.

It was obvious that members of the Press were not invited to this excursion - this seemed more like an exclusive rendezvous for Maribel and Som.

"Now, the assignment gets tougher. There will be armed bodyguards surrounding Maribel and Som – I'll have to find a way in and remain incognito to capture it all on film. I will quickly have to think of another disguise, as the Press is clearly not invited to this romantic outing."

Dwight could do little about his pudgy constitution and the birthmark and had to rely on other distracting elements like wigs, mustaches, beards and headgear to throw people off his scent. In the trunk of his car, Dwight always carried a valise full of such paraphernalia, which came in handy when he had to undergo a quick transformation.

But transform into what?

Maribel and Som were headed to The Chapultepec any moment now and Dwight had to act fast. As the sight and smell of food stimulated Dwight's brain cells into action, he wandered into a crowded restaurant, popular with tourists.

A quick burger, fries and coke, once again did the trick – Dwight decided that he would transform into an elderly American tourist with a cane. With his Bowler hat, wig, bushy whiskers, a flowing beard and a cane, Dwight was sure that Som would not recognize him.

Dwight was less concerned about Maribel spotting him, "Maribel is infatuated with her Somcito - she will definitely not be paying any attention to an elderly Gringo tourist. There are droves of tourists at the Chapultepec and Maribel's guards are less likely to be suspicious of an old man with a cane. I am brilliant. Viva Dwight!"

****

The historic Chapultepec Castle was located on top of the Chapultepec Hill in Mexico City's Chapultepec Park, one of the largest urban parks in the Western hemisphere. The Aztecs built a residence for their rulers here. Following the Spanish conquest, a summer palace came to be built in this spot. In the 1860s, Emperor Maximilian renovated and rebuilt the Castle, which remained the official residence of the presidents until 1940, when it became a museum.

Maximilian also embellished the surrounding park — this *'Bosque'* or Forest, is an important historical and cultural landmark and *a vital ecological green space, replenishing the oxygen in the Greater Mexico City.*

They say the way to a man's heart is through his stomach, but Som was no ordinary man. Maribel felt that the way to Som's heart was to take him on excursions of historical landmarks and have him feast his eyes on Mexico's rich cultural legacy.

Luckily for Maribel, Mexico City and its environs were replete with many such marvels.

Maribel's first stop in her seduction of Som was the historic Chapultepec Castle, sitting on the top of a hill.

The twelve rooms reflecting the opulent residence of Emperor Maximilian held a bounty of treasures, including a collection of exquisite furniture from the Colonial Era, as well as ancient manuscripts and works of art.

The Chapultepec Castle, being a major tourist attraction, was teeming with visitors. Maribel's arrival there with Som and a bevy of bodyguards raised quite a few eyebrows.

Som was in heaven absorbing the history and the beauty of the palace and its green exterior.

Dwight's disguise as an elderly American tourist worked pretty well. With his Bowler hat, wig, bushy mustache, flowing beard and cane, Dwight looked the part of the white-haired Grandpa and was able to get fairly close to Maribel and Som.

Unfortunately for Dwight, Maribel had brought along Oscar, Nacho and two additional bodyguards; together, this quartet formed an impenetrable human fortress, which surrounded Maribel and Som at all times. Dwight thus had a tough time getting a closeup shot of the couple - his pictures seemed to mostly capture the heads of the four bodyguards, rather than his intended targets.

To Dwight's great distress, Som repeated his behavior of the previous day at the Medical History Museum. He scrutinized each and every item at The Chapultepec Castle and asked Maribel lots of probing questions. Maribel was more than eager to provide Som with detailed answers, hoping that this would bring her closer to her *amorcito*.

As the afternoon rolled on, Oscar, Nacho and the two bodyguards were getting quite tired of this elaborate history lesson! Museums and historical artifacts were not their thing.

Besides, they did not feel safe spending this much time in a crowded museum teeming with tourists.

As Dwight was playing the 'Old Gringo Tourist', he tried his best to keep up appearances. But as Som stopped and studied every single item in the museum in great depth, it was becoming increasingly awkward for Dwight to hang around in close proximity to Som.

As Dwight had brought along an unwieldy cane as part of his disguise, he had to hold and operate his heavy camera with one hand, which now began to hurt.

After a couple of hours rolled by, Oscar, Nacho and the two bodyguards began to view Dwight with suspicion. Was this old man following them?

There were several odd things about this old man – his camera seemed to be rather unwieldy for an elderly tourist to be lugging along. Also, he seemed to be unusually agile for his age and there were times when he did not seem to be needing his cane at all!

But the oddest thing of all was that this old man seemed to be interested in the very same objects as Som was. Finally, it was unusual for an old man to have this much stamina and take these many photographs in a small museum.

Poor Dwight! He had not filmed a single romantic moment - so far, his photos and videos had captured more of the bodyguards than the 'couple in love', who seemed to be engaged in a riveting discussion of Mexican history, from the beginning of time to the present day!

As time went on, Dwight sensed danger. The facial expressions and the body language of Maribel's bodyguards looked ominous. Dwight knew that he had to exit the museum immediately.

Rather than get caught and face dire consequences from this menacing quartet, Dwight ran out of The Chapultepec and quickly dumped his cane, wig, Bowler hat, mustache and beard into the trunk of his car and changed jackets.

Now, the ever-hopeful Dwight waited outside the museum at the foot of the hill, as something romantic might still happen in the beautiful *Paseo de Reforma.*

****

Som and Maribel remained inside the museum until closing time. When the couple emerged, surrounded by their bodyguard quartet, Dwight was ready, having fortified himself with a coke and some potato chips.

This time, Maribel took Som on a leisurely stroll along the beautiful *Paseo de Reforma.* Maribel's bodyguards surrounded them in a close formation.

Dwight tailed Som and Maribel from a safe distance, capturing their stroll with his telephoto lens.

Finally, the long stroll ended with Maribel and Som entering a fancy bar for a drink.

Dwight slipped a crisp twenty-dollar greenback to a waiter to be seated close to the couple behind a partition. Now, Dwight ordered his favorite cerveza and listened in.

Som was telling Maribel about a Xavier, "Maribel, last Fall, Xavier was my Savior! He saved me from that odious man who wanted to throw out my precious books. And Xavier pulled it off with a night of Salsa dancing. The Salsa night was a roaring success."

"Really? So, *amorcito*, you know how to dance Salsa? That's simply divine. Let's call up this Xavier and go for a night of Salsa. *Vamos a bailar!* Let's go dancing!"

An elated Maribel made Som call Xavier from her phone. Xavier was game - the Salsa night in Mexico City was on.

And the action was going to be at Club Cielo.

Chapter 15
Salsa Night in Mexico City!

Dwight sat up with a jolt. He couldn't believe what he had just heard, "What? The World's most unlikely Romeo and Maribel are going for a night of Salsa dancing? And a Xavier is coming along too? This must be that same Xavier from the library - the Boss is not going to like this one bit. Maribel gallivanting about in Mexico City with Som is bad enough, but now, there is a Xavier joining in. I still have trouble believing that this Som guy can dance salsa. During the day, he is an utterly boring man with a museum fetish, but maybe, at night, he magically transforms into a Casanova."

And so, poor Dwight showed up bright and early at Club Cielo and slipped some crisp US dollar bills to the doorman and the head waiter, to secure a nice table at the mezzanine level, with an unobstructed view of the dance floor.

At 11 PM, Som entered with Maribel, who was accompanied by Oscar and Nacho. Following them was a handsome young man with a bevy of giggling girls on each arm – Dwight guessed that this must be the great Xavier. But that wasn't the end of it. Tía Thelma and Tío Bernardo were also part of this elite gathering.

From his vantage point, Dwight had an excellent view of the cozy booth which seated this congregation – Dwight had generously tipped all the right people in Club Cielo to make sure that Maribel and company would end up precisely at this very spot. Dwight had cleverly planted some bugs inside the flower-vase for picking up the audio feed from this table.

As Dwight's camera began rolling from the mezzanine level, the music started. Dwight was poised to take pictures of

Som and Maribel dancing salsa but what ensued did not follow the script.

Xavier grabbed Maribel and whisked her off to the dance floor for a round of salsa and cumbia. Xavier was an excellent dancer and Maribel did not complain. It had been a really long while since Maribel had been in the arms of a tall, dark and handsome man, dancing to the sensual Latin rhythms. Maribel let go of her inhibitions and danced with reckless abandon!

Som was not faring too badly either – the four girls who had walked in with Xavier, kept Som busy on the dance floor. Som was not the best salsa dancer, but he was good at the Chachachá. So, Som improvised, adapting his cool Chachachá moves to the Salsa beat.

The music changed to a fast merengue and now, Som and Xavier switched partners. Now, Som had Maribel in his arms and Xavier tended to his four girls. As other boys in Club Cielo asked the four girls to dance, Maribel ended up dancing with both Som and Xavier for a good stretch.

Then, came another switch of partners. This time, Som ended up with Tía Thelma and Maribel danced with Tío Bernardo.

Now, Tía Thelma was a whole lot heavier than Som and liked the man to give her a strong lead – if the man's lead did not meet her expectations, Tía Thelma resorted to back-leading the man and commanding him to execute the steps.

Tía Thelma felt that Som was *too restrained* in his dancing and needed to loosen up. She said to Som, "Dip me now! Then, lift me and swing me in a circle, and dip me again!"

A startled Som tried to follow her edict – things worked perfectly the first time around.

An excited Tía Thelma asked Som for an encore. And another and another.

Tía Thelma was a warm-hearted, lovable person to talk to and interact with, but lifting her up into the air was no easy task for an ordinary man. Tía Thelma had studied ballet in her youth and even performed a few times with her partner, Paco. The youthful and athletic Paco was well built with great muscles and had no trouble lifting the then nimble Thelma.

Unfortunately, the Tía Thelma of today, was no longer the nimble lass of those foregone days, and Som found this out the hard way. In the fourth round of the 'Dip and Lift' maneuver, things did not go so well.

As Som was unable to execute the 'Dip and Lift' maneuver to Tía Thelma's satisfaction, Tía Thelma decided to back-lead him into this complex sequence of steps, resulting in a great big fall for Som, with Tía Thelma landing on top of him.

Som was pinned to the dance floor, with the entire weight of Tía Thelma upon him. As Tía Thelma disengaged, Maribel and Xavier ran over to Som, trying to help him up.

But Som seemed to be frozen and unable to move. He broke into a strange babble, "Where am I? I can't seem to move. I am in another galaxy! I am seeing red and blue stars. There is a big black void. Now, I see pink and purple stars."

Xavier laughed, "You just had a great big fall, amigo. Sorry to disappoint you - you are not in a far-away galaxy. This is just Club Cielo in good old Mexico City and you are seeing the revolving lights of the dance floor."

"I know what the boy needs. Coming right up." cried Tío Bernardo, running up to the bar and ordering one of his special concoctions.

This special cocktail called for a mix of tequila, rum, vodka, Kahlua, sambuca, vermouth and whisky!

When the stunned bartender raised his eyebrows at this most unusual request, Tío Bernardo assured him that it was for medicinal purposes and urgently needed to heal an injured man and bring him back to life.

Tío Bernardo took one big gulp of his special concoction to ensure that it was just right, then, poured the rest of it down Som's throat.

Tío Bernardo was right. His special cocktail turned Som into a high-octane dancer, with boundless energy and enthusiasm. Som now effortlessly managed Tía Thelma's 'Dip and Lift' sequence with Maribel and the four other girls. An ecstatic Maribel asked Xavier to do the same 'Dip and Lift' sequence, which he executed to perfection.

****

While Tío Bernardo was resuscitating Som back to life and everyone was hovering around Som, Dwight was munching on a giant bowl of nachos. Yet again, this munching stimulated Dwight's brain cells into action and Dwight came up with a brilliant idea!

Dwight always carried a big wad of crisp US dollar bills on such outings – he now slipped a twenty to a happy waiter, telling him to keep his eye on Maribel and Som, while Dwight slipped out to the parking lot of Club Cielo, to implement his great plan.

This time, Dwight planted a GPS tracker and listening device in Tío Bernardo's cab. Now, Tío Bernardo's '*mula*', as the old man fondly referred to it, was Dwight's best friend! It would tell him where exactly Som was headed on any given day and record and relay 'any and all' conversations in Tío Bernardo's cab. And if Tía Thelma had any urgent messages for Tío Bernardo, Dwight would hear them too.

Feeling immensely pleased with himself, Dwight treated himself to a tequila shot and watched the frenzied dancing down below.

The unbridled Salsa dancing continued on to 4 AM – much to the relief of an exhausted Dwight, Som and Maribel parted ways. Som, Xavier and Tía Thelma left in Tío Bernardo's cab, while Maribel and her entourage returned to her bungalow.

****

Dwight came back to his hotel room, grabbed a cerveza and began to view the Club Cielo Salsa video. In the footage that Dwight had shot, Maribel seemed to be having the time of her life dancing salsa with both Som and Xavier.

Dwight knew Alonso would not be pleased. Dwight was supposed to keep an eye on Maribel and any man she was out with.

Dwight's workload, it seemed, had just doubled!

Dwight forwarded his report and the video to Alonso and waited for his next move.

Chapter 16
A Call to Adolphus!

The following morning, Dwight was on top of the world – the GPS tracker and audio bug in Tío Bernardo's *'mula'* were working like a charm and Dwight could hear Tío Bernardo's conversations clearly.

Luckily for Dwight, Maribel had slept in - no rendezvous had been set for that morning.

Dwight chuckled with glee when Tía Thelma called Tío Bernardo on his cell, as he was driving his cab. Tía Thelma was up on all the latest developments and excitedly shared them with her husband.

It appeared that Som was having a massive hangover from Tío Bernardo's curative cocktail. Señorita Maribel was a little out of it too and wanted to get a facial and a massage, so she would not be meeting Som that day. But there were big plans for the following day, when Señorita Maribel would be taking Som to see the Pyramids of the Sun and the Moon in Teotihuacan.

Dwight was immensely pleased with himself for planting those handy devices in Tío Bernardo's cab. This move had made life so much easier for Dwight - here he was, in the comfort of his own room, sipping his tequila sunrise and getting the whole scoop without missing a beat.

"I am brilliant! My idea of bugging Tío Bernardo's cab was pure genius. Thanks to this great man, Som is having the hangover of a lifetime. And Maribel is in no shape to venture out today either. This is a great day – I'll will now be able to get some much-needed rest and catch up on my sleep."

****

Sadly, Dwight's plans to have a good sleep were rudely interrupted by the ringing of the phone. It was Alonso calling.

Alonso was frothing at the mouth. He had spent hours staring at the video footage from The Chapultepec and the Salsa night at Club Cielo. The Chapultepec segment was dull and boring, but the Salsa segment was utterly infuriating. Maribel was in a dancing frenzy with not one, but two men! Besides the idiot Som that Alonso so despised, there was now another younger man in the picture. This Xavier was tall, dark and handsome and just the kind of guy that Alonso hated the most.

Not only was Maribel dancing with these two men, but she also had the nerve to send Alonso her 'Pic of the Day', showing her standing in front of a skyscraper in Toronto's Bay Street, pretending to be busy at work.

"Dwight, I don't like this one bit. Maribel is taunting me with her phony Toronto pics, sending me one a day, pretending to be working there, while she is living it up with this Som and Xavier! I want 24-hour surveillance on both now. You may get reinforcements if needed. Money is no object."

Dwight was badly in need of some sleep but could see that Alonso was terribly upset. The Boss now wanted 24-hour surveillance on two subjects - the assignment had just become much more complicated.

Keeping up with Som alone had been utterly exhausting - now, there was also a Xavier thrown into the equation! This Xavier was young and agile and probably a lot sharper than Som, so Dwight would have to think his strategy through carefully.

There was a pizzeria right across from the small hotel Dwight was staying in. Dwight always stayed at this establishment when he visited Mexico City - they asked no questions and let Dwight stay for however long as he chose to. As Dwight paid cash up-front and all of it in US dollars and was also generous with the tips, the staff in the hotel were more than eager to serve their favorite guest, Señor Dwight.

This ideally located hotel was close to a taqueria, a local pub, a pizzeria and several friendly restaurants and all Dwight had to do was tell the front desk what he wanted and he would get it pronto.

Dwight ordered two extra-large pepperoni and cheese pizzas and a big pot of steaming hot coffee to get his brain cells going.

As the pizzas and the coffee kicked in, the solution presented itself.

Dwight needed help - he could not tackle this duo of Som and Xavier all by himself. He needed Adolphus.

****

Dwight knew Adolphus was not the brightest, but he was family. He could trust the boy – Adolphus would not steal, do drugs, or run off with a woman. Another point in Adolphus' favor was that Adolphus did not like to do any independent thinking and asked few questions.

Adolphus was able to comply with basic commands like "Drive from point A to point B, tail subject 'X' and tell Uncle Dwight where he went, or take pictures of subject 'X' and bring them back to Uncle Dwight."

The fact that Adolphus did not like to 'think' and simply obeyed his commands, suited Dwight fine. The less the boy knew the better. Adolphus did love his beer though and after he'd had a few, he had a tendency to become loose-lipped; so, Dwight kept the details of a mission to a bare minimum and gave Adolphus simple instructions, so that Adolphus couldn't mess up.

As Adolphus was generally clueless about money, banks, credit cards and such, Dwight handed over Adolphus' earnings to his mother Eunice. As Adolphus lived with his mother, he did not have to worry about rent and bills.

Having Adolphus in his employ was not Dwight's idea, but one forced upon him by the persuasive Eunice. As Adolphus had flunked school and been fired from every job he had tried, Eunice had dumped Adolphus on Dwight, who couldn't say no to his sister.

But having Adolphus on an assignment was also a source of intense stress for Dwight. Any number of things could happen with Adolphus on the job. And the goof-ups were different each time.

For instance, one time, Adolphus was to tail someone and tell Dwight where the subject was going. Adolphus suddenly walked up to this subject and declared, "Ha ha, you'll never guess who I am. I am Adolphus Rex and I am hot on your trail."

Luckily for Dwight, most people dismissed these surprise pronouncements of Adolphus as the words of a crazy person and moved on without paying any attention.

Another time, Dwight and Adolphus were hiding behind a bush and taking pictures of two bad guys who were dealing in stolen electronics. At that very moment, Adolphus happened to spot an ice cream van and had the sudden urge for some mocha ice cream, so, he yelled out for the ice cream van to stop and chased after it, blowing Dwight's cover.

In Dwight's hotel room, there was an icon of 'The Virgen of Guadalupe' – Dwight bowed and asked for her blessings, as he was about to enlist Adolphus on this Mexico mission.

Dwight went on to book a flight for Adolphus to Mexico City for that very evening and sent the flight details to Eunice, texting her that he needed Adolphus in Mexico City. He also wired a thousand dollars to Eunice to hand over to Adolphus.

****

An hour later, the phone rang. Eunice sounded elated, "Dwight, it's real nice of you to want to show my Adolphus around Mexico. This will be his first trip abroad. I got the pocket money you sent him too. That's wonderful. It will be a nice holiday for my boy. Wish you had called me yesterday though. Adolphus has gone fishing. I don't know when he's coming back."

Dwight clenched his teeth in exasperation. He could feel a throbbing headache coming on.

"Eunice, please listen to me carefully. *I did not send the ticket and the money for a holiday in Mexico.* I need Adolphus here immediately, for an important assignment. Go find your son wherever he is and put him on that plane. He had better show up here right away, if he wants to keep his job!"

"Don't you take that tone with me. My poor Adolphus needed a break, so, he has gone fishing. He will be back when he is back."

"Eunice, why don't you tell your Adolphus to go fishing some other time? He never catches a thing anyway. I am sure

Mexico City will be a lot more exciting than his fishing expedition."

"Adolphus forgot his phone here at home. Adolphus will call you when he is good and ready. Bye."

****

Thinking about Adolphus usually ushered in three predictable symptoms in Dwight – this *triad* included heartburn, headache, or a combination of heartburn and headache. The heartburn-headache combo was the one that Dwight dreaded the most, as the headache remedy usually ended up worsening his heartburn.

This time, Dwight was afflicted with the headache, which increased in severity as the day progressed.

Late in the afternoon, that much awaited call from Adolphus finally came.

Dwight gave his nephew clear instructions, "Adolphus, your Mama will hand you a ticket to fly to Mexico City, along with your passport and a thousand bucks. She will drive you to the airport, get you checked-in and give you your boarding pass. All you need to do is go through the security check and once that is over, go to your gate and board the plane. Whatever you do, don't lose your passport, ticket and the boarding pass. The passport looks like a little book – please don't scribble on it or tear pages from it! When you land here, give me a call from the airport. Think you can handle that?"

Adolphus replied in the affirmative.

After speaking to Adolphus, Dwight ordered another pot of coffee and donuts and popped two aspirins.

Dwight's plan was taking shape - Dwight would go to Teotihuacan to keep track of Maribel and Som, on their visit to the Pyramids of The Sun and The Moon. Adolphus meanwhile, would monitor Xavier's movements in Mexico City.

Dwight's throbbing headache increased in intensity a few notches thinking of Adolphus tailing Xavier. At least, Som was like an absentminded professor who could perhaps be fooled, but this Xavier guy was sharp and Adolphus would need to keep his distance.

Well after midnight, Dwight got a call from Adolphus announcing that he had made it to Mexico City.

"Uncle Dwight, this is so exciting. Imagine me, Adolphus Rex, in Mexico City, on my first ever foreign adventure - I think I am going to like this place. Like Bond, I am ready for action - which '007' would you say looks most like me? You know what, why don't I mosey on and get myself acquainted with this town? Let me have a look around, get a feel for things, then I'll see you at the hotel."

"Adolphus, you stay put right where you are. Uncle Dwight will be over in a jiffy to get you."

Dwight prayed again to The Virgen of Guadalupe and jumped in his car.

Luckily, traffic was light and Dwight reached the airport without a hitch.

Dwight heaved a huge sigh of relief when he spotted Adolphus standing there with a giant sombrero, colorful poncho and cowboy boots.

"Hola, Uncle Dwight! Do you like my new outfit? I got me this getup to blend in with the locals. I think I fit right in."

Dwight thought Adolphus looked like a ridiculous buffoon, but kept his opinion to himself. He outlined the plan for the following day and went over it several times.

Finally, Adolphus decided that he had heard enough.

"Okay, okay, I got it. This Xavier guy lives in Colonia Reloj. I am to follow him wherever he goes and stick to him like glue. Is that all? How come you get to have all the fun seeing pyramids and things and I get to tail this Xavier guy? I think I deserve a more challenging assignment, Uncle Dwight. Why don't you let me chase after the lovebirds and you take on this Xavier?"

Dwight convinced Adolphus to stick with the Mexico City assignment by pointing out its significant merits, "Adolphus, do you want to climb 248 steps to the top of one pyramid, then, repeat the climb with a smaller pyramid? Do you want to spend the entire day on one sandwich and one measly soda? In Teotihuacan, you will do all of the above. In Mexico City, there is no climbing to do and you can enjoy tacos and gorditas to your heart's content!"

Adolphus said no more.

Dwight gave him a brief outline of 'who was who' in this love story and emphasized how important it was to get the best photos and videos of Xavier for the Boss, Don Alonso.

Two more pizzas and some hours later, Dwight felt that Adolphus had achieved a reasonable grasp of his assignment.

An exhausted Dwight had his two hours of sleep and got ready for his adventure in Teotihuacan.

Chapter 17
Off to The Pyramids of The Sun and The Moon!

Within an hour's drive from the sprawling metropolis of Mexico City lies Teotihuacan, one of the greatest archeological wonders of the world. The mighty pyramids of Teotihuacan are a testament to this City's glorious past, which remains shrouded in mystery and myth.

Maribel had rightly surmised that an expedition of this nature would be of immense interest to Som. Bright and early in the morning, Maribel and Som, accompanied by Maribel's usual entourage of Nacho and Oscar, headed for Teotihuacan.

Dwight decided to go as the journalist from the 'Eat more and Eat well Society' of El Paso. This was the premise under which he had been to Maribel's Press Event cum lunch. Teotihuacan being such a Mecca for tourists, no one would be surprised to see an American journalist taking in its glory. Dwight took his best camera along, to capture the video and audio on this glorious expedition.

Dwight had also brought along a *special surprise* for Som. For things to go according to plan, Dwight would have to 'accidentally bump' into Som in Teotihuacan, feign admiration for the great Chef Som, then, present this surprise item to him!

As Maribel and her entourage were heading for this archeological adventure, Dwight was following along, a few cars behind.

Maribel gave Som some historical details about their destination, "In Nahuatl, the name 'Teotihuacan' implies 'a place where men became gods'. Teotihuacan was designated as a UNESCO World heritage site in 1987. The city was inhabited from 100 BC to about 700 AD. So, why was this glorious City abandoned around 700 AD? Was it famine or drought forcing migration or was it an external invasion? We don't really know the answer."

Maribel chuckled, "*Amor*, as you have studied many languages, Nahuatl might interest you! Nahuatl, the language of the Aztecs, uses the '*tl*' sound as a single consonant. Do you want me to find you a tutor for Nahuatl?"

Som laughed, "I am having enough trouble mastering Spanish. I don't want to multiply my troubles by jumping into Nahuatl! Tía Thelma is my Spanish tutor. The twins want to teach me too. Oh, I almost forgot. Xavier says hello. Xavier is heading back to Toronto today – his extended Christmas holidays are over. I am really going to miss him."

"WHAT? Xavier is going back to Toronto today? Ah, if only I had known, I would have organized a send-off for him yesterday!"

Poor Dwight! *What a cruel twist of fate that he was not in possession of this bombshell news about Xavier, when he summoned Adolphus to Mexico.* Had Dwight known that Xavier was returning to Toronto, he would have managed the Som assignment all on his own, saved his thousand bucks plus the airfare for Adolphus, but most of all, avoided bringing that airhead Adolphus to Mexico.

But now, the die was cast and Dwight would have to cope with all the headaches and heartburn that Adolphus provoked.

****

The town of San Juan Teotihuacan was easily accessible by road, being about 50 km Northeast of Mexico City. Soon, Som found himself in the heart of the great metropolis that once flourished here.

The ancient Teotihuacan covered more than 20 sq km, and was divided into quarters by two great avenues that met near the "Citadel", a group of buildings in a large square complex, with its four walls being about 400 meters long and a series of platforms crowned with pyramids, enclosing a huge open space with the "Temple of Quetzalcoatl".

Maribel explained, "The main north-south avenue, which is 40 m wide, stretching some 2 km south from the Pyramid of the Moon to the Citadel and beyond, is the famous "Avenue of the Dead". It was so named by the Aztecs, who encountered this city in ruins and thought that the many mounds that flanked this avenue were tombs of former kings and priests!"

Maribel went on, "Religion occupied a central position in Teotihuacan many gods were worshipped here, including the Rain God, the Water Goddess, and 'Quetzalcoatl', the Feathered Serpent God!"

As Maribel and Som were admiring the decorations on the walls of the Temple of Quetzalcoatl with its striking sculptures of 'Feathered serpents', a cry broke out from beyond the walls of this mighty Temple.

"Señorita Maribel, Chef Som, *que sorpresa!* What a wonderful surprise! Imagine bumping into you here, in this Aztec temple."

A startled Maribel and Som turned to localize the source of this cry.

"Ah yes, I remember now. You were one of the journalists who attended my Press event. What a small world! Did you enjoy Chef Som's lunch? Which organization do you represent?"

"Chef's Som's lunch was divine! Señorita Maribel, I am proud to represent the 'Eat more and Eat well Society' of El Paso. And Chef Som's recipes are just what we are looking for. They fit our motto perfectly. Chef Som, please permit me to present to you, this token of our appreciation. Please accept this amulet of 'Quetzalcoatl, The Feathered Serpent', on behalf of the 'Eat more and Eat well Society' of El Paso. I meant to present it to you at the Press Event the other day, but never got the chance."

Without waiting for Som's response, Dwight deftly planted this curious looking amulet on Som, who accepted it with a big smile.

Som thanked Dwight, "I will cherish this beautiful gift from you and your Society. I hope this amulet will bring me good fortune."

"This amulet is supposed to bring good fortune not only to the one who wears it, but also to the one who bestows it!" replied Dwight with a twinkle in his eye.

****

The amulet, which hung on a secure chain around Som's neck, looked rather colorful and attractive.

While Som felt empowered with the amulet of Quetzalcoatl, Dwight was on top of the world for having planted *a high-quality listening device and GPS tracker* on Som, cleverly hidden inside the Feathered Serpent!

Now, Dwight could pick up the audio from Som from anywhere, as long as Som wore this lucky amulet. He would also know Som's exact location, thanks to the GPS tracker inside it.

Feeling rather victorious, Dwight now followed Som and Maribel at a safe distance. The next destination was the Pyramid of the Sun, some 65 meters tall and standing on a square base of over 220 meters on each side. The façade of Pyramid of the Sun faced west - according to an ancient legend, the setting Sun changes into a jaguar, which sinks into the darkness of the night.

Maribel, being in fine physical shape, scaled the 248 steps to the top of this pyramid in no time at all. Som struggled his way to the top, and eventually made it.

Oscar and Nacho grudgingly followed. They *were not fond of* such assignments which involved tall monuments and a lot of climbing.

The one who was in some serious trouble was Dwight.

On the ascent to top of this Pyramid, Dwight began to feel queasy. He was half-way up when he was hit with a major panic attack, "If I look down, I feel dizzy! I don't feel so good. I hope I don't fall down. What an unceremonious end that would be. At least, I should make it to the top. Only a loser would climb a pyramid half-way up and turn back."

Poor Dwight struggled his way up to the summit, where Som was standing, proudly wearing his glorious amulet.

Reaching the summit was most rewarding, as everyone got a breathtaking view of the complex and the Pyramid of the Moon.

The athletic Maribel was the first to race down the steps of the pyramid. She stood there laughing at the men. Som, Nacho, Oscar and Dwight were all in bad shape, crawling at a snail's pace.

For Som, the going down part was even more tricky – he had to avoid looking down and focus on taking one step at a time. He somehow made it and heaved a huge sigh of relief.

Dwight was the last to come down. As he was slowly making his way down the final few steps, Som waved to him from below, "I think your amulet is bringing me good luck! I can feel it! See you at the Pyramid of the Moon!"

****

Som and Maribel were back on the 'Avenue of the Dead', heading northward to the Pyramid of the Moon, the second largest structure in the complex. Although the shorter of the two, it looked almost as tall as the Pyramid of the Sun, as it was set on higher ground.

Finally, Dwight crawled back to earth from the Pyramid of the Sun. From his earphones, he could pick up the audio feed from the lucky amulet that he had gifted to Som.

"I don't believe this guy. *He is repeating his museum behavior all over again!* He is exploring every nook and cranny of this giant complex. Thank God I planted this device, otherwise, I would be a dead man!"

Som was indeed having the time of his life taking in the rich artistic legacy of Teotihuacan, strolling through the Palace of the Jaguars, the Temple of the Feathered Snails, and the Palace of Quetzal Butterfly. Som ended on a high note with the 'Tepantitla', with its walls depicting the Rain God Tlaloc and housing Teotihuacan's famous fresco, "Paradise of Tlaloc".

Maribel was happy to see her *amorcito* in such high spirits. She decided that the way to Som's heart was more Quetzalcoatl.

"*Amorcito*, I'll take you to the Museum of Anthropology tomorrow. You can learn about all the Aztec and the Mayan Gods and deities there. It will be sheer heaven!"

Som thanked Maribel for her generous offer.

Oscar and Nacho exchanged doleful glances - they hated museums with a passion.

A triumphant Dwight smiled – he could now afford to skip these boring museum outings; the amulet of the Feathered Serpent would do the work for him.

Chapter 18
Adolphus gets to work!

While Dwight was busy climbing pyramids in Teotihuacan, Adolphus woke up and treated himself to a hearty breakfast of fried eggs and chilaquiles.

Dwight had given him a photo of Xavier and his address in Colonia Reloj. Adolphus' assignment was straightforward – he was to follow this Xavier guy and take lots of pics.

The fact that he was in Mexico City on his first ever 'overseas mission', made Adolphus feel mighty important. The wad of money Uncle Dwight had handed to him, added to this feeling of euphoria.

"Uncle Dwight keeps giving me boring tasks like following a guy or gal and shooting some pictures. It's time he realized that I, Adolphus Rex, am capable of so much more. I am going to read through this Maribel file and see what Uncle Dwight has dug up so far."

Adolphus opened Uncle Dwight's briefcase and located the Maribel file.

Adolphus knew well enough that Uncle Dwight *did not like to have people rummaging through his personal files!* Uncle Dwight was always rather tight-lipped about assignments and shared the minimum details with Adolphus, who was kept informed strictly on a 'need-to-know' basis.

Adolphus knew he was doing the *forbidden* thing by going through Uncle Dwight's files, but reasoned with himself, "The time has come for 'Adolphus Rex' to be an equal partner, rather than a simple errand boy – it's about time Uncle Dwight cut me in on some real action!"

Adolphus learned several noteworthy details from Uncle Dwight's notes – he now knew where Som lived in Toronto and which libraries Som worked in. He also found the contact details for Don Alonso.

Adolphus now asked the hotel manager to 'hurry up and get him a car immediately'. Then, he stuffed the one grand his uncle had given him into his pocket, and took off in pursuit of Xavier.

****

Xavier had extended his Christmas holidays well into January, but now, it was time to head back to Toronto and get back to work.

Xavier said goodbye to his parents, Tía Thelma and the twins. Numerous heartbroken girls also came by to bid a tearful farewell to their *'galan'*. When the goodbyes were finally over, Tío Bernardo drove Xavier to the airport for his flight to Toronto.

As Adolphus followed Xavier, he had a strange feeling - the route seemed awfully familiar!

"Why do I get the feeling I've been on this road before? Hey, this cabbie is breaking all the speed limits, but maybe, that's how they drive in this country. I like it. It seems this Xavier guy is going somewhere in a great hurry. So, where is he off to anyway?"

That question was answered in short order as Tío Bernardo's cab pulled up to the airport. Xavier hugged his uncle, said goodbye and entered the airport.

"Why is this guy entering the airport? Hmmm, what do I do now? Oh heck, I'll follow him to the end of the world if I have to. I don't have time to put this car in parking, so I'll have to leave it here. They will probably tow it, but Uncle Dwight can take care of the bill."

****

Adolphus chased Xavier into the airport and positioned himself right behind Xavier, who was now at the Air Canada counter.

"Where are you flying today, Sir?" asked the pretty girl behind the counter, flashing Xavier a big smile.

Xavier replied that he was heading for Toronto.

Adolphus, who had never heard of this place, quickly tried to scribble it down on his palm.

Xavier thanked the pretty girl and left with his boarding pass, heading towards the Security Check.

Now, it was Adolphus' turn. When the pretty girl asked him where he was flying to, Adolphus flashed a big smile and replied, "Torto, Miss. I am a man on a mission."

"May I have your ticket, Sir?" asked the puzzled girl.

Seeing that he had no ticket, the girl walked with him to another counter and asked him for his destination again.

Adolphus again replied that he was flying to 'Torto' and was informed that a destination did not exist.

"Ah, I was just kidding. I am going to the same place as the guy you were just talking to. He is my buddy."

As Adolphus had his American passport and his US dollars, there were no questions asked - Adolphus secured a seat on the flight to Toronto.

After the security check, Xavier got himself a coffee and sat down.

A strange looking man with severe acne and thick glasses walked up to Xavier and flashed a big smile, showing off his gold-capped incisors. He sat beside Xavier and introduced himself, "Hi there, I am Adolphus Rex. I am a man on a mission."

A startled Xavier quickly excused himself and headed towards the washroom to get away from this curious stranger.

"What a strange-looking guy! He must be high on something." mumbled Xavier to himself.

As Xavier was leaving the washroom, he ran into the man, yet again.

At that moment, there was a boarding call for Xavier's flight. Xavier seized this opportunity to get away from this weird guy.

To Xavier's great surprise, the weird guy was on that same flight to Toronto, but luckily, seated all the way to the back. When the nearly five-hour-long flight came to an end, Xavier, who was seated in the front, bolted out of the plane, heading for the immigration checkpoint. As he stood in line, Xavier saw the weird guy waving to him from afar.

Xavier, who normally was not rattled even by an earthquake, was a little shaken. A strange guy was following him all the way from Mexico City, smiling at him and waving to him. Xavier wanted to get far away from this character, so he hopped into a cab and quickly disappeared into the evening traffic.

****

Now, Canada has immigration and customs forms to fill upon arrival – the form is bilingual with one side in English and the other side in French and asks for details such as 'Expected duration of stay in Canada, countries visited recently, address in Canada, purpose of the trip, how much alcohol one was bringing into the country, was one visiting a farm soon and so forth'.

The form confused the heck out of Adolphus, especially the French half.

Adolphus struggled with the form for a long time and finally managed to scribble something down. Adolphus decided that he would claim to be a tourist and give Som's address as his place of stay.

By the time Adolphus made his way through immigration and customs, he had totally lost track of Xavier. It was also evening and it was getting dark. Not knowing what to do and where to stay, Adolphus hopped into a cab and gave the cabbie Som's address. Forty-five minutes later, the cab pulled up in front of a high-rise building in downtown Toronto.

'That will be forty-seven dollars, Sir." said the cabbie.

Adolphus handed him a fifty US dollar bill.

"That is forty-seven Canadian, Sir. How much change did you want back?"

"Keep it all, cabbie!" replied Adolphus, hopping out of the cab.

"So, Canada has its own dollars. How interesting! But the cabbie didn't seem to mind my US dollars. This must be a super friendly country. I shall have some beer and pizza and think of my next move. Uncle Dwight will be so pleased with my initiative." Adolphus said to himself, wandering into a restaurant, right across from Som's residence.

Chapter 19
Uncle Dwight, I am in Toronto!

Adolphus ordered an extra-large pepperoni pizza topped with four kinds of cheese and mushrooms and two pints of beer.

When he paid with another fifty US dollar bill and said to keep the change, the owner of the restaurant, a Mr. Pintauro, was all smiles.

"Oh, Thank you, Sir. Thank you so very much. Anything else I can do for you?"

"Everyone seems to like my American dollars very much. This Canada must be a really friendly country. Everyone is so nice to me here – I should come here more often." thought Adolphus.

Adolphus asked Mr. Pintauro if there was a hotel nearby, for the night.

It so happened that there was one right next door.

Mr. Pintauro took an instant liking to this amicable tourist, who was flashing US dollars and leaving enormous tips! He immediately made a call to the hotel and found Adolphus a room. He told Adolphus to come back to 'Pintauro's Pub and Restaurant' for breakfast, lunch and dinner.

Now that he had a room for the night and a friendly pub to come back to, Adolphus turned his attention to the mission at hand. Having lost Xavier's trail, Adolphus now stood in front of Som's apartment building, contemplating his next move.

****

At that very moment, Mrs. Moon and Winston stepped out for their evening walk.

The events that followed took even Mrs. Moon by surprise.

Winston began circling around Adolphus, wagging his tail! Adolphus, likewise, reciprocated the feeling and patted Winston.

Mrs. Moon gasped and stared in disbelief. Winston taking a liking to another human being was a rare event.

"Hey Mister, Winston likes you. You must be someone special to win Winston's heart!" cried Mrs. Moon.

"Hello Winston, I am Adolphus Rex. I am a man on a mission."

"And what might that be, Adolphus Rex?"

"Well, Ma'am, I am on the trail of a fugitive named Xavier, who is the friend of Som Shekar, who lives in this very building. You wouldn't happen to know this Xavier, would you?"

"No, but I do know this Som Shekar and can tell you everything about him – maybe, I could even help you find this Xavier fellow."

"Much obliged Ma'am. Thank you kindly." cried Adolphus, taking off his sombrero and bowing to Mrs. Moon.

Mrs. Moon and Adolphus ambled over to Pintauro's Pub, where Mrs. Moon was happy to relate many juicy stories about Som, over a few beers.

Adolphus for his part, told Mrs. Moon all about Uncle Dwight and himself, about Don Alonso and the Maribel-Som affair, and how Xavier had now entered into the picture.

"I am here to keep tabs on this Xavier. Mrs. Moon, you know what? *I am going to bypass Uncle Dwight and send my pictures of Xavier directly to Don Alonso.* That should teach Uncle Dwight a good lesson. I am tired of being taken for granted by Uncle Dwight."

Mrs. Moon was enjoying the evening immensely. The 'Som soap opera' had now taken an exciting new turn and Mrs. Moon, was now playing a vital role in it.

Mrs. Moon promised to help Adolphus locate Xavier; she then ran over to Landlord Wu to bring him up to date.

Mrs. Moon could hardly contain her excitement, "You'll never believe what I just found out. This Maribel is going after both our SS and this Xavier guy and she has an insanely jealous husband. I am having breakfast with Adolphus tomorrow. We need to be on the lookout for this Xavier and help poor Adolphus."

****

Back in his hotel, Adolphus felt tremendously pleased with himself and picked up his phone to call Uncle Dwight.

"Uncle Dwight, I have big news for you. I am in Toronto, hot on the trail of this Xavier. I lost him at airport, but have made an important contact here in Toronto and hope to nab him soon. You will be proud of me, Uncle Dwight - my contact's name is Mrs. Moon and she is Som's neighbor. You couldn't get any closer to Som than that. And guess what, I saved you a heap of trouble by directly sending Xavier's pictures to Don Alonso! He must be looking at them as we speak. Isn't that brilliant? I think I deserve a raise."

Dwight was driving back from Teotihuacan when Adolphus called. Adolphus' words sent him into a state of shock, causing him to almost hit another car!

"WHAT? WHAT DID YOU SAY? What do you mean, you are in Toronto? I didn't send you there, so, what the hell are you doing there? Who cares about Xavier if he is back in Canada, you idiot? And what do you mean, when you say you sent Xavier's pictures to Don Alonso?"

Before Adolphus could respond, Dwight had another call coming in. It was the Boss calling. The Boss seemed to have lost it completely!

"Dwight, your operative Adolphus, just sent me countless pictures of this Xavier and the insides of an airplane! This Xavier seems to be heading somewhere on this plane. I can't make out the other passengers… What is the meaning of this? Is Maribel with him? Is she on that plane? What's going on?"

"Señora Maribel is right here in Mexico City, Boss. I am following her car as we speak. She is not with Xavier. Call you with the latest, as soon as I get off the highway."

A shaken Dwight exited the highway and quickly drove back to his hotel. He now had a throbbing headache and the beginnings of another Adolphus-related symptom, heartburn.

Little did he know of the utter chaos that he was about to walk into.

Chapter 20
The Feathered Serpent comes through!

The minute Dwight stepped foot into his hotel, he encountered the hotel manager, Señor Santos, in a state of profound agitation.

A visibly upset Señor Santos informed Dwight that his nephew Adolphus had demanded a car urgently and insisted on taking Señor Santos' own car, but the car had been unceremoniously ditched at the airport and had now been impounded. Señor Santos had spent a most unpleasant afternoon with airport security and the cops and the matter was still not cleared up.

Señor Santos declared that he was looking at one whopper of a '*multa*' – one hell of a hefty fine plus additional penalties, thanks to Adolphus.

Dwight apologized profusely to Señor Santos and offered to pay for any and all costs associated with this unpleasant business and handed him a big wad of US dollars for his troubles.

****

Dwight now called Don Alonso to bring him up to speed on the Som-Maribel saga, "Boss, things are looking good. I have planted a GPS and audio device on this Som, so we'll know exactly where he is and what he is saying. Today, Señora Maribel and Som were visiting Teotihuacan and I was right there with them. Tomorrow, Señora Maribel is taking Som to the Museum of Anthropology. Knowing this guy as I do, he will spend the whole day there, staring at every item in the museum. I will have access to the GPS and audio and know exactly where he is every step of the way, so, we are well covered. Everything is under control."

"Then, why am I being flooded with pictures of this Xavier guy and the insides of a plane?"

Dwight badly wanted to know the answer to that very question himself.

Damned Adolphus! This was all his doing!

Dwight had to make something up to 'justify' these inexplicable actions of Adolphus to Alonso.

"Boss, this morning, it was unclear to me which way the wind was blowing and I wanted to keep all bases covered. So, I had my operative tail this Xavier, while I took on Som. My operative wanted to make absolutely sure that this Xavier guy was traveling alone and Señora Maribel was not giving us the slip and cleverly sneaking away with him. Now, we know for sure that Señora Maribel is definitely in Mexico City, so, it's all A-OK! She will visit the Museum of Anthropology tomorrow, so you have nothing to worry about!"

Upon hearing that Maribel's next outing would be to the Museum of Anthropology, Alonso felt much calmer. Also, the devilishly handsome Xavier was now safely out of the way in Toronto.

****

After Alonso hung up, Dwight reached for both his antacids and his aspirin. Before he gave a piece of his mind to that idiot Adolphus, Dwight needed to make an important decision.

"Now that Xavier is out of the way, should I ship Adolphus back to Texas or have him join me here in Mexico City? It has only been four days on the Som mission, but already, I feel utterly drained. I could really use the extra help, but I can't cope with Adolphus. Adolphus gives me headaches and ulcers. Sending him back to Texas may be the wrong decision, but that's what I am going with."

Having made up his mind, Dwight felt a huge sense of relief. Dwight knew he would get an earful from Eunice and a whole lot of whining from Adolphus, but his mind was made up. The Adolphus debacle had already cost Dwight over three grand – the full brunt of the damage and the final tally would be known when Señor Santos' car, which had been ditched at the airport entrance by Adolphus, could be finally retrieved and returned to its owner.

Dwight booked a flight for Adolphus back to Texas and proceeded to deliver the bad news, "Because of your moronic actions, Señor Santos is in tears – his car has been impounded and God only knows when he will get it back. Señor Santos is a dear friend – now, because of you, I have lost face and have to make reparations. It's costing me a bundle and I have a good mind to take it out of your pay! I don't know what you are doing in Toronto hobnobbing with that Mrs. Moon, but your holiday is over. *Adiós* Adolphus! Happy travels."

With Adolphus now out of the picture, Dwight felt a huge weight lift off his shoulders. After ordering a juicy steak for dinner, Dwight reflected on his day, "With this lucky amulet that I managed to plant on Som, I now have the upper hand. This amulet will be my eyes and ears tomorrow. I can stay in the comfort of my room and hear all about the exciting finds in the Museum of Anthropology."

****

The next morning, Dwight ordered a sumptuous breakfast in his hotel room and listened in, as Som embarked on his exhaustive tour of the Museum of Anthropology, asking Maribel lots of questions about Mexico and its history.

The amulet of the 'Feathered Serpent' was indeed paying handsome dividends for Dwight - he could hear every word clearly!

True to form, Som stayed at the museum until closing time, after which Maribel took him to the famous 'Porrúa' bookstore, right across from the museum. This was followed by a visit to 'Librerías Gandhi', a bookstore named after the great Mahatma Gandhi.

Being in his element in these bookstores, Som stumbled upon some marvelous books on Mayan ruins by the celebrated American explorer, John Lloyd Stephens, with illustrations by his companion, the Englishman Frederick Catherwood, who happened to be an accomplished artist and an architect.

The two had set out in 1839 on an ambitious expedition to explore the mysteries of the Maya, returning back for a second round in 1841- they described in exquisite detail some 44 Mayan sites. The details of their glorious expeditions appeared in illustrated treatises, with a detailed account by John Lloyd Stephens, accompanied by the drawings and lithographs of Frederick Catherwood.

It was this magnificent set of books that had caught Som's eye at the bookstore and sent him into a rapture.

Som got himself both volumes of the 'Incidents of Travel in Central America, Chiapas, and Yucatan' by John Lloyd Stephens, as well as Catherwood's priceless art folio entitled, 'Views of Ancient Monuments in Central America, Chiapas and Yucatan'. Maribel gifted to Som some additional books about the Maya.

****

Enjoying a coffee at a local Café, Som began to browse through these enchanting books.

"Maribel, these Catherwood lithographs are absolutely stunning! Did you know, my father is an artist too? He is at this very moment in Venice, capturing its magnificent architecture in his drawings, etchings and lithographs. Seeing Frederick Catherwood's beautiful illustrations, *I regret not taking my sketchbook along, when we visited Teotihuacan.* I don't know if I would be any good with architectural drawings, but I should at least give it a try while I am in this enchanting land."

"I think that is a fantastic idea, *amorcito*. But why stop at Teotihuacan? Why not go to some of the same ruins that this explorer-artist duo visited? I have planned a few more events for you in Mexico City, after which we could visit any of the ruins detailed in these books and you can draw and paint to your heart's content! Now, about tomorrow… I have a special surprise for you! I think you will be especially thrilled with tomorrow's itinerary."

"Oh, what might that be?"

"Being a librarian, I am sure you will enjoy a visit to the iconic libraries of Mexico City, which is what we are doing tomorrow. And the day after tomorrow, we shall visit the Anahuacalli Diego Rivera Museum, which is in right in your backyard in Colonia Reloj. And not far from it, is the Frida Kahlo Museum, which will certainly interest you as an artist. Then, we shall head over to some spice markets and talk about your series for the magazine. Seeing how great your first demo went, I think we should have you do another demo. How do you feel about that?"

"It all sounds wonderful. I can't wait to go to the libraries of Mexico City. Now, about the articles, I have been giving much thought to the theme of my series – I have a few ideas in mind. I think I will write about the 'history of food' and the evolution of a particular dish. I may also do another series about spices and herbs – here, I can incorporate my drawings too."

Maribel took Som to a few more bookstores – Som ended the day on a high note, having acquired many wonderful books to take home to Toronto.

For her part, Maribel felt quite pleased with the progress she had made on the Som front – Som was no ordinary man and the way to his heart was through books, monuments, and museums!

Poor Nacho and Oscar were bored out of their minds accompanying Señorita Maribel on these 'Som outings' – their hearts sank upon hearing that the next item on the list was a visit to the many libraries in Mexico City.

The happiest man in Mexico City that evening was Dwight. For Dwight, things were looking up – Adolphus was on a flight back to Texas and Dwight's headache and heartburn were gone. Best of all, the amulet of the Feathered Serpent that Dwight had gifted to Som, was working like a charm!

Chapter 21
The Feathered Serpent runs amok!

That evening, back in Tía Thelma's house, Som called Priyanka to give her a detailed account of his Mexico adventures thus far, especially his new acquisitions of the books on Mayan ruins by John Lloyd Stephens, with masterful illustrations by Frederick Catherwood.

"Priyanka, I wish you could come over right away. We could visit each and every one of these Mayan ruins detailed in these books. I am dying to do some architectural drawings of these majestic monuments - I don't know if I'll be any good though. Tomorrow, I will be visiting the libraries in Mexico City. There is so much to see in this wonderful country."

Priyanka promised to come over as soon as she could get out of her assignment.

Som proudly showed Tía Thelma and the twins the books he had just bought. The twins thought the books were nice, but were more intrigued by the colorful amulet around Som's neck and wondered if they could wear it. Som gladly parted with the amulet, but a great big fight broke out about who would get to wear it first. Som arbitrated the dispute and drew up a detailed schedule for Ivan and Adelita, for the use of this precious amulet.

Poor Dwight was blissfully *unaware that the amulet of the Feathered Serpent had now changed hands!*

Dwight was in a celebratory mood, patting himself on the back, ordering his favorite ice cream, caramel flan and churros (fried dough sticks), "How very clever of me to have come up with this amulet – now, I can skip the library outing of tomorrow. Nothing romantic could possibly happen inside a library – I am sure this guy will look at every book in every library in Mexico City. I do feel kind of sorry for Oscar and Nacho – imagine being trapped in a library with Som… how utterly excruciating!"

The following day, Maribel took Som on an unforgettable tour of some of the most renowned libraries in Mexico City. The tour included the National Library of Mexico, the Central library at UNAM (the University), and the Vasconcelos Library. For Som, stepping into the majestic National Library which was founded in 1867, was an intensely emotional experience.

While Som was in heaven browsing through these precious collections, Dwight was having a decidedly *bizarre* morning!

Dwight was hearing strange voices emanating from his precious amulet – instead of picking up the dialogue between Som and Maribel, the amulet seemed to broadcasting the cackle and chatter of kids!

A puzzled Dwight listened hard for a few hours, utterly baffled, "Wonder what went wrong! The amulet was working perfectly fine yesterday, but it seems to be picking up some really strange signals today. Maybe there is a school trip to the library and the kids' voices are drowning Som's, but can't imagine kids being trapped in a library for this long… something is definitely off."

The mystery deepened further, when the GPS trail led Dwight to a kindergarten!

Dwight knew Som was balmy, but couldn't fathom what would motivate this crazy librarian to visit a kindergarten, when there was so much else to do in this exciting city.

It was then that Dwight saw the twins on a seesaw, playing with their little friends. To his horror, Dwight spotted something else hanging off the neck of Adelita – the amulet of the Feathered Serpent!

"Gosh! I now know why I've been hearing strange things all morning. Little Adelita is wearing the amulet instead of Som. This guy is really going to give me a heart attack. Has he gifted my amulet to the twins? I hope not. How do I get him to wear it again?"

As the kids were under the watchful eye of a teacher, Dwight decided that it would be too risky to approach them to find out how they came to be in possession of his precious amulet. Without the amulet, Dwight would have to tail Som and Maribel the hard way, by waiting outside Maribel's bungalow and following her limo.

Dwight knew Som was inside some library in Mexico City, but which one? It would be a fool's errand to wander over to the various libraries in search of Som.

Dwight had to concede defeat for the day.

****

When Maribel left her bungalow the following morning, Dwight was ready, keeping a few paces behind. After Maribel picked up Som, the first stop was the Anahuacalli Museum.

Without his lucky amulet to aid him, Dwight had to resort to his disguises once more. This time, he opted for a cowboy outfit with cowboy boots and spurs, a cowboy hat, jeans and a leather belt with a metal buckle.

Just minutes from Tía Thelma's house was the Anahuacalli Museum, which housed 2,000 pieces from the personal collection of the great Mexican muralist, Diego Rivera. Diego Rivera's priceless collection included over 50,000 pieces from the pre-Hispanic era.

This unique museum, envisioned as 'A Temple of the Arts' by Diego Rivera, was completed after the artist's death, by architects Juan O'Gorman and Heriberto Pagelson and Diego Rivera's daughter, Ruth.

Inspired by Mesoamerican structures and incorporating Mayan and other influences, this unique monument was carved out of volcanic stone.

Som looked in awe as he stepped inside this remarkable pyramidal structure made of black volcanic stone from the Xitle volcano, which had erupted some 2000 years ago in the southwestern part of Mexico City – *these volcanic rocks had been extracted from the very terrain where the museum now stood!*

Amongst the many museum offerings, were large-scale sketches for some of Diego Rivera's famous murals.

Cowboy Dwight felt a little out of place in this Mesoamerican sanctum and tried to keep a low profile, quietly capturing pictures and videos of Som and Maribel.

Oscar and Nacho were in no mood for Mesoamerican art and patiently endured Som's fixation on each and every piece.

Maribel then took Som to '*La Casa Azul*' or 'The Blue House', with its brilliant cobalt blue walls. This was the very house where the legendary artist Frida Kahlo had grown up and spent most of her life in. Years later, Frida Kahlo lived here with her husband Diego Rivera.

This beautiful Blue House, a few short miles away from Anahuacalli, now housed the Frida Kahlo Museum and featured artwork by Frida Kahlo, Diego Rivera and other artists.

"Maribel, this is unbelievable - within minutes from Xavier's house, lies a magnificent museum made out of volcanic stone, with an extraordinary collection of Mesoamerican art. And some three miles from it, lies the enchanting Blue House of Frida Kahlo. What a great gift to the Mexican People from Diego Rivera and Frida Kahlo! I would give anything to live here in Colonia Reloj – it is a far cry from my apartment in that concrete jungle I live in. Xavier comes from such a historic city. Oh, how I envy the people who live here!" cried Som.

Maribel was pleased to see Som in such high spirits, "As an artist, you will also enjoy the *'Palacio de Bellas Artes'*. It houses some of the most famous Mexican murals and is a must see. But today, we shall visit the spice markets – they will blow your mind away."

****

After leaving the Blue House, the action moved to 'Mercado de Coyoacán', followed by 'Mercado La Merced', one of the largest food markets in Mexico City.

For Dwight, this meant another quick costume change – he transformed once again into the journalist from El Paso for this mission. As the market was crowded, Dwight could easily blend in and observe Som and Maribel from afar.

Oscar and Nacho hated crowded markets bustling with people; in their view, these were infinitely worse than libraries and museums in terms of providing security to Señorita Maribel. This Som mission had been the most trying one from their perspective - the guy was dragging Señorita Maribel into all sorts of crowded places. Oscar and Nacho strongly disapproved of such outings, but did not dare to speak up and voice their objections.

The market-hopping continued on with gusto, with visits also to 'Mercado de Jamaica', 'Mercado de Medellín' and 'Mercado San Juan'.

The sight of food markets made Dwight extremely hungry – he was deeply upset with Som for not stopping for a bite in this gastronomic paradise. Instead, Som was busy shopping for his next cooking demo, which was scheduled for the following morning.

By the end of the day, Som managed to amass an impressive assortment of spices, herbs, chilis, vegetables and fruits for his demo.

Maribel dropped Som off at Tía Thelma's and rushed off to do the Press invites for Chef Som's 'Dips, Chips and Smoothies'.

Som returned from his day's adventures in high spirits, thinking about the menu for this exciting event.

Dwight had only one wish for that evening – he hoped the amulet of the Feathered Serpent would change hands once again and bring him good luck in the days to come.

Chapter 22
Chef Som's Dips, Chips and Smoothies!

As the reporter from the 'Eat more and Eat well Society' of El Paso, Dwight received a press invite from Maribel for Chef Som's 'Dips, Chips and Smoothies' event.

Maribel also extended an invitation to Tía Thelma, Tío Bernardo and the twins. Remembering the happy faces the last time Tío Bernardo had played bartender, Maribel invited him for an encore. Maribel also wondered if Tía Thelma would mind being Som's assistant yet again.

Tía Thelma and Tío Bernardo were more than happy to oblige.

The following morning, Som, Tía Thelma, Tío Bernardo and the twins hopped into Maribel's limo and headed to her bungalow for Som's next culinary adventure.

Dwight was at the bungalow bright and early, as were other members of the Press.

To Dwight's immense regret, the twins Ivan and Adelita, were still in possession of the amulet of the Feathered Serpent.

There was a new face in the Press core – a Mr. Barron Colt, freelance photographer from England, had joined in.

Barron Colt was none other than 'Barracuda', who had finally made it to the very doorstep of Maribel!

After months of snooping around, Barracuda had just learned of Maribel and Som's current whereabouts. Wasting no time, Barracuda hopped on the next plane to Mexico City, hoping for some juicy scoop to send to Alonso.

Barracuda's modus operandi was to start with a teaser and slowly squeeze his victim into submission. Now in his late sixties, Barracuda was hoping that this could be his farewell assignment with a handsome payoff, which would enable him to retire comfortably in his coffee plantation in Costa Rica.

Having captured that passionate 'Maribel Kiss' in Toronto, Barracuda had high expectations for this Som event. Unlike the formal Toronto Gala, Som and Maribel were in a more intimate setting this time, in Maribel's bungalow no less, where Champagne was flowing freely.

Adding to this festive spirit, were the 'potent cocktails' dispensed by a most affable bartender, who went by the name of Tío Bernardo.

Maribel welcomed the guests and the Press and introduced Chef Som, who started off with a still-life painting of an eggplant, plantains and a colorful array of Mexican chilis.

As the painting evolved, Tío Bernardo's cocktails kept the audience in high spirits and agog with expectation.

Dwight and Barracuda were probably the only two members of the Press who sagely avoided Tío Bernardo's potent elixirs! They kept their eyes glued to Maribel and Som.

When the still-life painting was finished, the audience broke into a big applause. Now, Chef Som got down to the serious business of making his dips, chips and smoothies.

****

The ambitious menu included baked plantain chips, baked sweet potato chips, baked eggplant chips, Tirokafteri (Greek feta dip), chickpeas hummus, apple-pear-kale-ginger-lemon-flax smoothie, tomato-kale-celery-carrot-lemon smoothie, mango yogurt smoothie, roasted eggplant-red pepper-olives dip and spicy wholewheat tortilla chips.

As Som labored over his precious creations, Tía Thelma helped with chopping the vegetables and getting the smoothies and dips into the blender.

For Dwight, who by now was used to Som and his ways, the events of the morning were par for the course.

Barracuda on the other hand, was in a state of utter shock – he had just blown two thousand dollars on this special trip to Mexico City, giving up a most lucrative assignment in Paris, all in the hopes of getting some compromising pictures of Som and Maribel. This wacky 'art expo cum culinary fest' was not at all what Barracuda had envisioned.

As the morning progressed, Barracuda felt a veil of gloom descending upon him - if this was the extent of the 'illicit affair' between Som and Maribel, then all he had in his arsenal were those Toronto pics of the 'Maribel Kiss'. For Barracuda, the dream of that handsome payoff from Alonso was fast evaporating.

"Why didn't I go to Paris? Why ever did I come here of all places? I am now left with a few measly photos from that Toronto Gala and need to act soon! This guy is too weird to be a passionate lover - there is nothing to photograph here. This is really depressing. I'm going to head over to Tío Bernardo's bar and get plastered." lamented Barracuda.

****

Unlike Barracuda who was down in the dumps, Chef Som was flying high. But with so many items on the menu, Chef Som was in for a few surprises himself, some of his own doing, and the rest thanks to Tía Thelma!

Having overbaked his spicy wholewheat tortilla chips, Som ended up with chips which were hard as rock! Som's rock-hard chips were especially popular with the twins, who began to play with them, calling them, 'Som Frisbees'!

This impromptu 'Frisbee' game caught on with some of the more inebriated guests enjoying Tío Bernardo's cocktails.

Interest in 'Som Frisbees' grew, as more participants joined in the game.

Tía Thelma explained to these guests that these 'Som Frisbees' had been specifically created by Chef Som as 'playthings' for the kids.

"This is utterly humiliating - the twins and the guests are playing 'Frisbee' with my chips. The guests will definitely end up breaking their teeth if they bite into these chips. There is no time to bake a fresh batch. What to do now? But wait, what if I dip them in a sauce to soften them up? Yes, that might work. I'll make a sweet, sour and spicy yogurt dip with tamarind, sugar and chili powder – if I soak my chips in this dip, they will be part crunchy and part soft. That's brilliant! My chips can be salvaged and there will be no broken teeth."

Having rescued his wholewheat tortilla chips, an upbeat Som worked on the remainder of his menu – once he was done preparing a dish, he handed it to Tía Thelma for plating.

Tía Thelma tasted Som's creations and quietly went about making some *'fine adjustments'* of her own!

In doing so, Tía Thelma quite radically altered the original taste of Chef Som's masterpieces – the 'Tirokafteri' now had the fiery habanero rather than the roasted red pepper, elevating the 'heat' level up by several notches.

Tía Thelma also augmented the amount of Tahini in the hummus, making it super yummy.

As for the smoothies, Tía Thelma felt that they needed a *boost* in the form of some spirits and told her husband to take care of this little matter.

Som was blissfully unaware of these interventions by Tía Thelma.

Finally, it was time to dig in. But before these delicacies were served to the guests, Maribel had one more surprise for everyone. Som's watercolor painting of the plantains, eggplant and the colorful chilis was auctioned off to the highest bidder. The lucky winner got the 'Chef Som original' and a year's worth of subscription to Maribel's health food magazine.

Having imbibed several of Tío Bernardo's potent cocktails, the guests and the Press were all in a happy state and extremely appreciative of Chef Som's creations. The Smoothies turned out to be especially popular, as they had Tío Bernardo's magic touch with a good shot of Tequila and Rum. Som's spicy tortilla chips in the sweet and sour yogurt sauce, the fiery hot Tirokafteri with habanero and the deliciously creamy hummus, were all in high demand.

Once again, Chef Som was a big hit with the guests and the Press.

Dwight looked longingly at the amulet around little Adelita's neck and prayed for its quick return to its intended owner.

Barracuda consoled himself by imbibing a great many of Tío Bernardo's cocktails. He had given up a great assignment in Paris to come to this strangest of events; he would now have to accelerate his plan to extract a payoff from Alonso.

Chapter 23
Mexico, here I come!

That evening was marked by an extraordinary constellation of occurrences, some that were random and happening entirely by chance, some that were deliberate and intentional acts, and some that were unintended consequences of unfortunate slip-ups.

In the 'random' group, was the unexpected arrival of Rocky in Mexico City. Som's brother-in-law Rocky was married to Som's sister Trisha. Rocky was a real estate tycoon, always on the lookout for new prospects. Having just concluded a whopping real estate deal in Ecuador, Rocky was eager to get cracking on his next big project.

Hearing through the grapevine that Som was friends with Maribel Villanueva, wife of the oil-magnate Alonso Villanueva and daughter of the wealthy Don Geronimo, Rocky wanted to seize this golden opportunity to further his real estate aspirations in Central and South America. Rocky was hoping to charm Maribel and talk his way into meeting her fabulously rich husband and her even more powerful father. Rocky had arrived solo – his wife Trisha was in no mood for the overcrowded and congested Mexico City and had opted for the beaches of Acapulco.

In the 'intended and deliberate acts' category, belonged the doings of Barracuda, who was downing a bottle of tequila and listening to some doleful Mariachi music. A sense of utter despair had come over Barracuda after attending Som's 'Dips, Chips and Smoothies' event, leading him to make the drastic move of demanding half a million US dollars from Alonso, as a payoff to keep his silence and not sell the 'Maribel Kiss' pics to a tabloid.

In his inebriated state, Barracuda had also appended a postscript, "I am here at the party with the lovebirds. Barracuda knows all!"

This regrettable error would soon come back to haunt Barracuda!

In the 'unintended consequences' category of occurrences of that fateful evening, were the doings of Maribel herself – having enjoyed one too many of Tío Bernardo's cocktails, Maribel had made a most unfortunate error. Instead of sending Alonso one of her Toronto skyscraper pics as she did each day, Maribel had mistakenly shared with Alonso, a picture of Som painting his still-life of the eggplant, plantains and chilis in her own garden, with the caption, "I just discovered the Artist of the Year! I'd love for you to meet him!"

Maribel had intended to send this picture to her friend Alana – unfortunately, Alonso's name followed right after Alana's name in Maribel's contact list and poor Maribel had clicked on the wrong name and pressed 'SEND'!

Barracuda's ultimatum and Maribel's taunting mail arrived simultaneously, sending Alonso right over the edge – Alonso decided that it was time to pay this duo a visit.

By sending that picture taken in her own garden, Maribel had declared to Alonso that she was now in Mexico City, so it would be entirely reasonable for Alonso to meet his wife and get to know this 'Artist of the Year' that she had discovered. Why, Maribel herself had intimated that she'd love for him to meet the guy!

By hinting that he was 'with the lovebirds', Barracuda had inadvertently revealed his location - it made sense for Alonso to fly to Mexico City now, to see things with his own eyes, and snuff out the likes of Barracuda.

And so, Alonso simply hopped on his private jet and landed in Mexico City, at his usual penthouse suite at the Marriott.

****

For Som, who was blissfully unaware of these happenings, it was an evening to celebrate - his ambitious 'Dips, Chips and Smoothies' event had been a resounding hit.

Som sent Priyanka a detailed text about the goings-on of the day, including the surprise auction of his still life painting.

Eagerly awaiting Priyanka's call, Som picked up the travelogue of John Lloyd Stephens and gazed longingly at the spectacular architectural drawings by Frederick Catherwood, "I want to visit every one of the ruins detailed in this book. It is going to be an unbelievable adventure. Where should I go first? I want to draw them all. But will my drawings be any good? I seem to be okay at capturing an onion or a tomato on canvas, but will I be any good with monuments? According to this book, Frederick Catherwood used a camera lucida to project the outline of a monument on his canvas – I have no such tools. I am also short-sighted and things are kind of blurry at a distance, but hey, I could do my impressionist rendition of the ruins… I wish Priyanka would hurry up and get here soon. I can't wait to show her all of Mexico."

At that moment, the phone rang, bringing Som out of his reverie – feeling certain that it was his beloved Priyanka calling, a happy Som cried, "Hello my darling, how I have missed you!"

There was a chuckle from the other end, "Hello my darling, I've missed you more!"

Som was startled. Did Priyanka have a sore-throat? She sounded so different!

"Darling, are you okay? Do you have a sore-throat? Your voice sounds different – you must take something for it. I keep forgetting it is winter in Delhi. Is the smog bothering you? How is everything?"

There was another chuckle from the other end, "*Kullu Tamaam.* All A-OK!"

Som sat up, surprised. Priyanka did not usually speak to him in Arabic.

"Come right over, my darling!"

"Coming right over, Habibi. I am right here at the airport - just tell me where you are."

"WHAT? Priyanka, did you say you were at the airport? Oh darling, I am the happiest man on earth. Stay right there. Tío Bernardo and I will be right over to get you."

"Ha ha, I won't move an inch, I can't wait to see you. Come soon, Habibi, I've booked us a suite at the Marriott."

****

Som jumped into Tío Bernardo's cab and headed for the airport. But he felt strangely uneasy about the phone conversation he had just had. Priyanka did not usually address him as 'Habibi' – the only one in the family who habitually called him 'Habibi' was Rocky. Also, Priyanka would not have booked a hotel suite without consulting Som. Was this Rocky pulling a prank, masquerading as Priyanka? It must be

- that would explain why Priyanka's voice sounded so different! What was Rocky doing in Mexico City?

Rocky knew he was being a bad boy, leading Som on and pretending to be Priyanka on the phone. By way of apology for playing this practical joke, Rocky was planning to invite Som to join him at his luxury suite at The Marriott.

Som's suspicions came true – upon arrival at the airport, there stood Rocky, large as life, laughing his head off.

"I knew it was you, Rocky. In the beginning, you had me fooled, but when you signed off, I knew something was off."

"Ah, too bad you found me out, Habibi. But good news! I have booked a great suite at the Marriott – I invite you to join me."

"I am fine where I am – I love at staying at Tía Thelma's flat; this is her husband, Tío Bernardo. So, what brings you to Mexico City?"

"Oh, just some real estate matters. I hear you are working with Maribel Villanueva – wow, you are certainly moving in the big leagues now. I'd love to meet your Maribel!"

"Where is Trisha? Is she still in Quito?"

"Trisha hates Mexico City – she is off to Acapulco. Is Priyanka joining you?"

"Soon! I can't wait to take her to the Mayan ruins."

Dwight, who was sipping a margarita in his hotel room, took in this interesting exchange between Som and this new arrival, Rocky, from the bug he had planted in Tío Bernardo's cab.

"I wonder who this Rocky is and why he wants to meet Maribel. If he booked a suite at the Marriott, he is a man of means. I hope this doesn't mean more work for me." thought Dwight.

Dwight's musings were interrupted by the ringing of the phone. It was the Boss calling.

"Dwight, the plot thickens – Barracuda just declared war and wants his payoff; he says he was at the party with the lovebirds. Speaking of the lovebirds, guess who sent me a special picture today? My Maribel! My Maribel had the gall to send me a picture of this guy painting vegetables – she says he is her 'Artist of the Year' and she'd love for me to meet him. So, guess where I am, Dwight? I am in Mexico City, at my usual penthouse at The Marriott and am here to meet this 'Artist of the Year' and snuff out Barracuda. Meet me at the penthouse immediately - I want to see all the footage from today's party and the one before – Barracuda was there and we are going to put a face to the name. *Los voy a matar!* I am going to kill them both! Som and Barracuda, your days are numbered."

Chapter 24
The Artist of the Year!

Poor Dwight had been looking forward to a restful evening when Alonso called. This urgent summons by Alonso forced Dwight to drop everything, grab all of his video footage and notes, and head straight for the Marriott.

Dwight was not feeling so well – suddenly, things seemed to be spinning out of control. Barracuda had just declared war! And the flighty Maribel had sent Alonso a picture of Som in her garden and incited his wrath. Now, Alonso was in town and he was in an unforgiving mood.

"I have the footage of all the attendees at Maribel's two parties – it was pretty much the same crowd both times, but I should see if there were any new faces today - one of them must be Barracuda. The Boss sounds really upset – I guess, he has every right to be. Poor Maribel – I bet she has no idea of the storm that she had unleashed. And poor Som! Yes, the guy drives me crazy, but he is not the womanizer the Boss thinks he is. He loves museums, cooks weird stuff and draws even weirder things – the man is loco, but he is no Casanova. How do I convince the Boss that he is barking up the wrong tree?" muttered Dwight to himself.

When Dwight saw Alonso, it was not a pretty sight. Alonso's face was a deep hue of reddish purple and a vein throbbed in his temple. Alonso greeted Dwight and got down to the matter of the videos and photos immediately.

Alonso watched the complete video footage of the events of that morning. It started off with Som doing his still-life of the eggplant, plantains and chilis, then, immersing himself in his chips, dips and smoothies.

Alonso stared at the entire video in silence. Dwight stood by nervously, waiting for Alonso's reaction.

Alonso, thus far, had been sceptical when Dwight had sent him his daily reports, insisting that nothing exciting was going on between Som and Maribel. Having sat through the entirety of the video footage, Alonso was inclined to agree with Dwight.

The video seemed more like a comedy sketch from start to finish. Alonso burst out into fits of laughter, "Dwight, this guy is a kook – only a screwball would think of painting an eggplant, plantains and chilis, then, spend an entire morning making strange dips, chips and smoothies! How did they taste, anyway? Is he any good?"

"Boss, this guy somehow manages to pull it off – with his weird choice of ingredients, one would expect things to taste utterly horrible, but his creations are really quite tasty; I don't know how he does it."

"Everyone at this party seems to be happy and laughing."

"Oh, that's all thanks to Tío Bernardo's special cocktails – they really pack a punch! The Press just loves them. Señora Maribel is brilliant for getting this man in as her bartender. It's a great strategy to get the Press on her side and she is guaranteed a great review."

"Mmmm…. So, you say nothing is going on between this Som and Maribel?"

"I swear nothing's happening. This guy is extremely boring, but he can really tire you out - *don't ever step inside a museum or a monument with him! It's an utterly excruciating experience.*"

"Maribel is raving about him, calling him 'Artist of the Year'! I don't get it – what does Maribel see in him? Even if there is nothing is going on between them as you say, he must *still be punished* for kissing Maribel at that Gala. Nobody kisses my woman and gets off scot-free. That kiss brought in the likes of Barracuda and opened up a real Pandora's box, so the guy has got to pay. Guess what, I just thought of something… as this guy calls himself an artist, I am going to commission him to do some pieces for me - the art had better be to my liking, or else, heads will roll!"

Alonso's brow furrowed, "Dwight, coming to this Barracuda - I have been a patient man so far. But no more. I want you to nail this Barracuda - he is right here in one of your pictures, so, find him. Nobody messes with Alonso Villanueva!"

Chapter 25
A Big Surprise for Maribel!

The strange events of that evening were far from over.

As Dwight pored over the videos and photos from the two Som events to divine the identity of Barracuda, an anxious Alonso paced up and down, smoking a cigar, eagerly awaiting the verdict.

By the strangest of coincidences, Rocky's suite happened to be directly below Alonso's penthouse.

Rocky had invited Som and Tío Bernardo to his Marriott suite for drinks, to be followed by dinner at a nearby Italian restaurant. Before Som could say no, Tío Bernardo had quickly jumped in and accepted Rocky's invitation, leaving Som little choice but to go along.

Rocky, of course, was blissfully unaware that Alonso's penthouse suite was one floor up - the man that Rocky was dying to meet was directly overhead. At that very moment, Alonso happened to be standing in his balcony, impatiently waiting for Dwight's big reveal as to the identity of Barracuda. Had Rocky gone to his balcony and shouted out Alonso's name, Alonso would definitely have heard him and Rocky's wish might have been fulfilled.

Rocky poured a round of whisky for himself and his guests and began grilling Som about his collaboration with Maribel.

"Som, I can't believe it. You, who set the kitchen on fire in Toronto, have now become a celebrity chef and artist, all thanks to this Maribel! I would love to meet this brave soul who put her trust in your cooking. She really pulled off the impossible!"

Som nodded in agreement – he was indeed most indebted to Maribel for believing in him. His own family had made fun of his cooking, cruelly mocking him and laughing at his culinary creations, but not Maribel – Maribel had stood steadfastly by him through it all. She had introduced Som to the Press and the people. Thanks to Maribel, Som was now a respected chef and artist – people were even buying his painting in an art auction.

****

Meanwhile, in the penthouse suite right above, Dwight was busy reviewing the video footage from the two Som events.

"How much longer, Dwight?" asked Alonso impatiently.

"Getting there, Boss. Won't be long."

Alonso, tired of pacing up and down, decided to give Maribel a call and have a bit of fun. An impish grin came over his countenance as he greeted his wife, "*Amada mía*, my beloved Maribel! I am so thrilled to get your 'picture of the day' from your own bungalow. Darling, that can mean only one thing – your Toronto assignment is done and you are in wonderful *México*. Who is this wonderful 'Artist of the Year' that you have dug up? Does he do portraits? I want him to do one of you and me. My love, I can't wait to see you. I will join you tomorrow in Mexico City and you can introduce me to your artist."

Blood drained from Maribel's face as she came to realize her colossal error – she had sent the wrong picture to Alonso. How could she have been so careless? Now, Alonso was coming to Mexico City to meet her artist and have him do portraits of them. What an utter nightmare!

Alonso chuckled, "Darling, are you there? You are awfully quiet!"

"Oh yes, darling! I am so happy that you are coming. Of course, you will meet this artist. Darling, as far as I know, he does still-life paintings and dabbles in architecture – I don't know if he does portraits though."

"Maribel, tell your artist friend that Alonso Villanueva wants him to do a special portrait of Alonso and Maribel! And I won't take no for an answer. And you say he dabbles in architecture? That's just great. Tell your artist that I am also commissioning him to draw our glorious Mayan monuments. He shall be well compensated of course, but he had better do a good job – you know Alonso cannot stand mediocrity. I will see you tomorrow. *Buenas noches y dulces sueños, mi amor!*"

Alonso signed off with a big grin, wishing Maribel 'Goodnight and Sweet Dreams'. The thought of making Som sweat, doing a portrait of him and Maribel, had improved Alonso's mood considerably. Maribel had bragged about discovering the 'Artist of the Year' – now, this Som had better come through and do a portrait to Alonso's liking. It was going to be a lot of fun to go to the Mayan ruins with Som, point to something and command Som to draw it! And it would all be under the watchful eye of Alonso.

The trap was set – all Alonso had to do now was sit back, relax and enjoy the spectacle!

Chapter 26
Alonso plans his revenge!

Rocky's whole purpose in making this impromptu visit to Mexico City was to get to know the two powerful men in Maribel's life - her husband, Alonso Villanueva and her father, Don Geronimo. But to get to these two powerful men, Rocky would have to go through Maribel. And the person who held all the cards to gain entry into Maribel's world was Som.

Poor Rocky! Little did he know that directly above his suite at the Marriott, stood the majestic penthouse that housed the very man he was so eager to embrace.

Up in that very penthouse, Dwight was staring hard at the video clips and the countless photos from the two Som events – the goal was to find that fiend, Barracuda, who was present at the second event.

By poring over the guestlists and meticulously checking off each name against each face, Dwight finally settled on the most likely candidate.

The evidence pointed to one 'Barron Colt', who claimed to be an independent photographer from England.

"Boss, I am pretty sure it's this Englishman here. His name is Barron Colt – that's our Barracuda, in the flesh. And come to think of it, 'Barron Colt' even rhymes with 'Barracuda'! That's pretty clever, don't you think?"

Alonso stared long and hard at the image in front of him - Barracuda appeared to be an older, sophisticated gent, possibly in his sixties.

"This is no ordinary rogue – I think this Barracuda means business. If I don't pay up, he is going to go through with his threat. But I can make him sweat for his money and have some fun with it. Yes, Barracuda will get his money, but he's going to have to work for it."

Stumbling upon the identity of Barracuda put Alonso in a great mood – he poured a generous tequila shot for himself and another for Dwight and raised his glass in a toast, "Dwight, *I am going to greatly relish getting even with these two gentlemen!* This is my plan - I am going to invite both Som and Barracuda to accompany Maribel and myself to Chichen Itza and Uxmal, the two Mayan ruins I am very familiar with."

Alonso's face lit up with a big smile as he continued, "For Barracuda, I have an interesting game in mind – Barracuda will of course be hooked, as it will mean more bucks for him. In this game, I will designate various 'Rendezvous points' where Barracuda will get a mystery clue. The clues will be in the form of riddles that you will deliver to his cellphone, when he makes it to a designated 'Rendezvous point'. Barracuda will have to figure out these riddles, which would be based on the ruins of Uxmal and Chichen Itza. If Barracuda is successful in deciphering these riddles and making it out alive, I, Alonso Villanueva, will compensate him handsomely, doubling what he is asking for. On the other hand, if Barracuda were to fail, he would be a lost soul seeking that elusive fortune, wandering about the ruins of the Yucatan!"

Alonso chuckled, "Now for Som - I have thought of the perfect plan to exact my revenge and get even with Som. As Maribel bragged about her discovering the 'Artist of the Year', I am going to commission Som to do a portrait of 'Alonso and Maribel'. I shall also commission him to paint vignettes of Uxmal and Chichen Itza, with the 'stipulation' that should they should stack up against Frederick Catherwood's masterful renditions of the Yucatan! This is going to be loads of fun – I plan to watch Som closely while he is drawing these monuments. In short, between doing the portrait and drawing the monuments, I am pretty sure our Som will turn into a hopeless wreck - that will be his punishment for kissing Maribel!"

Dwight was relieved to see the Boss in such good humor after coming up with his masterplan – he was sure Barracuda would go for Alonso's crazy proposition, as there would be an extra five hundred grand in it for the taking.

Dwight felt kind of sorry for Som - thanks to Maribel's bragging and her careless slipup, Som had now been dragged into a tough spot with no escape. Even if Som did the best portrait and the best views of the monuments, art was a very subjective thing - the judge, jury and executioner in this case, all happened to be Alonso.

Alonso's plan seemed more like an elaborate setup to *torment* Som, rather than a deadly vendetta to 'do away' with him. It seemed to Dwight that Som, although in no mortal danger, might suffer a nervous breakdown or even lose his mind, attempting to draw portraits and monuments to Alonso's liking.

Dwight felt greatly relieved that Alonso would not be resorting to violence, when it came to Som and Barracuda. There would be no more exhausting expeditions to museums and monuments to tail Som – hereon, Som would be under the watchful eye of the Boss himself.

For Dwight, there was another veritable cause for celebration - having solved the mystery of Barracuda's identity, Dwight himself, was now a step closer to getting that big fat cheque from Alonso, for a job well done.

After Dwight departed, Alonso ordered himself a juicy steak and smiled. Revenge was going to be sweet and Alonso was going to savor every minute of it!

Chapter 27
Som's First Art Commission!

When Som got home from the Marriott, there were several urgent messages for him from Maribel.

"What's the matter, Maribel? You've left me seven messages! Is there something wrong?"

"Everything, *mi amor*. You are in big trouble! I am sorry I got you into this, but I can't get you out of it. I should have never come to Mexico. But wait, you were the one who came to Mexico, I just followed you. I don't see a way out of it now."

"Maribel, please calm down. I am not following you. Please tell me what is wrong. Why am I in big trouble?"

"It's all my fault, *amorcito*. I messed up today by sending the wrong picture to my husband Alonso. Now, he knows we are here in Mexico City. The picture was of you doing your still-life this morning; I added a caption saying, 'I just discovered the Artist of the Year, I'd love for you to meet him!' Alonso has decided to come over and meet you in person. He's coming tomorrow."

"I'd be most happy to meet your Alonso. I still don't understand why I am in trouble."

"Alonso wants you to do a portrait of him and me. He is also commissioning you to do vignettes of Uxmal and Chichen Itza."

"WHAT? THAT'S CRAZY! I am no portrait artist – I have never done portraits. For that matter, I have never done architectural drawings either – whatever gives him the idea that I can do any of it?"

"I might have blurted it out. Anyway, you can't refuse now!"

"What do you mean, I can't refuse? Doesn't Alonso know that I am a librarian who dabbles in art? I am passionate about art, but it is not my métier. I could probably take a stab at architectural drawing, but attempting a portrait would be totally out of my league. I will just explain to Alonso that I am not a portrait artist – I am sure he will understand."

"*Mi amor*, you don't know Alonso – he is obstinate and inflexible. Once he makes up his mind, there is no going back. He also has a fiery temper - no one dares to cross Alonso. Please do it for me, my love. You did a good-looking eggplant, plantain and chilis today and the other day, you did a good job with the zucchini, onion and tomato. How hard can it be to do a face? Just think of it as one of your vegetables and add a couple of eyes, a nose and a mouth to it and voilà, you've got your face!"

"Ha ha, that's a great suggestion, but it's not that easy. I can't take on something that I am clueless about. My dear Maribel, I don't want to mess up your portrait, so you will just have to explain to your Alonso and get me off the hook."

"I can't. We are stuck. Alonso is coming in tomorrow – I can hold him off for a couple of days but that's about it. Say, why don't you go to those bookstores I showed you and get a 'how-to' book? Or ask Tía Thelma and Tío Bernardo to get you one from the library. Sorry, my love, when Alonso makes up his mind, it's a done deal – there is nothing I can do to change his mind. By the way, as I mentioned, Alonso also wants you to do some vignettes of Uxmal and Chichen Itza and expects you to be *as good, if not better* than Frederick Catherwood."

Som's jaw dropped, "That's utterly insane! Frederick Catherwood was a professional illustrator – the best in the game. I am a total beginner and don't know if I'd be any good at all."

"But you have enough time to study those books that you bought and familiarize yourself with Catherwood's drawings, don't you? *Mi amor*, the best I can do is three days – I promise to keep Alonso busy for three days, so that you get time to prepare. *Suerte, mi amorcito,* I wish you lots of luck – now remember, I vouched for you. I said you were my 'Artist of the Year', so please don't let me down! I am sure you can do it. You are going to be great – I believe in you. *Ciao mi amor,* I have lots of things to organize before Alonso gets here."

With that, Maribel was gone.

Som thought he was losing his mind. This was crazy! Som wanted to call Priyanka and spill his guts, but couldn't reach her.

First, he had to get the scoop on this Alonso and his fiery temper.

Som had a long chat with Tía Thelma and Tío Bernardo about this strangest of conversations he had just had with Maribel.

"Tía Thelma, Tío Bernardo! Maribel said that Alonso has a fiery temper and he never takes no for an answer. Do you know anything about his man? *Isn't it strange that he would want me to do his portrait?* I don't even know the man and I have never done a 'portrait painting'. That's a job for a professional artist… I couldn't possibly learn it in three days. How can this man commission me to paint his portrait of all things? I am going to say no – Som is a free spirit. Som paints what he wants, when he wants!"

Tía Thelma and Tío Bernardo disagreed completely and broke into a passionate bilingual outburst in English and Spanish, describing the fiery temper of Alonso Villanueva and his intolerance for sloppiness and mediocrity.

Aunt Thelma cried, "Somcito, no one ever says 'NO' to the great Alonso Villanueva! So, end of discussion, period, *punto*. You should take it as a great honor that he is giving you this art commission. You say you have never done portraits? *No problema*, we will get books and videos for you to learn. Better still, I will introduce you to my cousin, Paco. Paco can do miracles with photographs - he can make marvelous paintings out of any photograph. Get Don Alonso and Señorita Maribel to pose here in your room – tell them it is your studio. Paco could hide behind the curtains and snap their photo. Don't show them the painting until it is finished. After each sitting, Paco can help you with the painting, using the photos to capture the likeness. As you will be working with oil painting, it is easy to make changes. Don't worry about a thing, Somcito. *Dios mío*, I can't believe Don Alonso and Señorita Maribel will be in our house, posing for you."

Tío Bernardo agreed with his wife, "Somcito, nobody ever says 'NO' to Don Alonso. At least, nobody that wants to stay alive! So, you accept his command with a smile and we'll get Paco to help you. Problem solved."

"This is getting out of control – did you know, Alonso is also taking me Uxmal and Chichen Itza so that I can draw the monuments that he wants? And get this – he wants my drawings to be as good if not better than Frederick Catherwood's drawings. The man is utterly mad, if you ask me. Frederick Catherwood was the greatest! I am just a novice. I am a nobody."

"Your problem, Somcito, is that you are too afraid. Be confident. Everything will work out fine. You are going to need assistants for this venture – the two of us and Paco shall be your assistants. Come, let us celebrate this great achievement – imagine getting an art commission from the great Don Alonso! *Felicidades* Somcito!" cried Tía Thelma, as Tío Bernardo poured a round of Mezcal for everyone.

Chapter 28
Portrait painting is not easy!

The next three days were frantic – Som got himself a bunch of 'how to' books to learn the basics of oil painting, portrait painting and architectural drawing. The material was staggering – it was a lot to take in and Som felt utterly overwhelmed.

Som studied Frederick Catherwood's exquisite illustrations and sighed, "Painting and drawing *cannot* be learned from books. What have I gotten myself into? How did it ever reach this point? These Catherwood drawings are spectacular – there is no way I can match this. And I have never drawn a face – what if my portrait bears no resemblance at all to Alonso and Maribel? I am in big trouble… I shall ask Priyanka if she is able to see a way out of this."

Priyanka broke into a hearty laugh when Som told her of his predicament, "Darling, artists usually have the opposite problem. They want art commissions and nobody gives it to them – you, my love, have one too many! Come to think of it, Maribel's suggestion is actually quite practical. We know you are good at painting vegetables, so it is just a matter of adding the eyes, ears, nose and a mouth. Just make sure Maribel doesn't end up looking like a squash - that might land you in big trouble!"

"Priyanka, this is no laughing matter – Maribel says Alonso has a fiery temper. And he can't stand mediocrity."

"Why do you assume that your work will be mediocre? Didn't Tía Thelma promise to have this Paco give you a hand? Get him to give you some pointers. I am sure it will all work out. I believe in you. I can't wait to see your portrait!"

****

And so, Som started his 'Portrait Painting 101' with Tía Thelma's cousin, Paco. Paco was a little guy with boundless energy. Paco was apparently self-taught and could do faces from photographs.

With Tía Thelma posing as their subject, Paco taught Som the basics of portraiture. Som marveled at the flexibility of oil painting and the ability to cover up the wrong stroke by simply painting over it.

After the three days went by, Alonso called Som and introduced himself, "Som, this is Alonso Villanueva, Maribel's husband. Maribel speaks most highly of you and has proclaimed you her 'Artist of the Year'. Now, I want to gift to my dear wife, a portrait of the two of us for our anniversary. I thought to myself, who better than Som, our 'Artist of the Year', for such an important assignment! There is also another project very dear to my heart - as you know, I am from the Yucatan and have fond childhood memories of growing up there. I want you to capture some vignettes of Uxmal and Chichen Itza for my art collection. We take off as soon as you finish the portrait - I shall take care of all the travel arrangements. You may bring along anyone you wish. I hope this will be the beginning of a long and beautiful friendship between us."

Som tried getting out of it by telling Alonso that he was a novice, but Alonso stood firm and wouldn't take no for an answer.

Finally, Som had no way out but to invite Alonso for the portrait session, "Alonso, for portraiture, I prefer to work in my studio, right here in Colonia Reloj. I invite you and Maribel to my studio tomorrow to start the portrait. Paco will be my assistant. Tía Thelma and Tío Bernardo are most eager to meet you - Maribel knows them well. Could you be here around eleven tomorrow morning? I imagine it will take us a few sittings."

"*Estupendo!* Great! *Hasta mañana,* Som."

****

After Alonso hung up, Som went into a panic. Tía Thelma and Tío Bernardo tried to calm him down, "Tomorrow will be a great day, Somcito. Two of the most famous people in Mexico will be right here in our house and you will be doing their portrait. Paco will help you, so you have nothing to worry about. Let us celebrate this great occasion!"

Tío Bernardo poured everyone his special 'celebratory cocktail' and insisted that Som have two of them, being the famous artist. Tío Bernardo's potent elixir calmed Som down considerably. The next morning, Alonso and Maribel arrived promptly at the accorded hour, with a beautiful bouquet of orchids and a bottle of Lindeman's chardonnay. Tía Thelma and Tío Bernardo were overcome with emotion upon seeing this celebrity couple in their home. Som introduced Paco, who seated the couple on the sofa for the portrait and adjusted the lighting.

Maribel was her usual pretty self with one notable difference – she had done something to her hair, which looked frizzy and stood up on its end, like in those science experiments with static electricity! Alonso also seemed to be sporting a similar hairdo. Alonso had a square jaw and a handlebar mustache - his well-toned muscles complemented his heavily tattooed neck and arms. Alonso was in an all-black outfit, while Maribel was in a short, tight red dress with a plunging neckline. Maribel also had on big silver earrings, chains and bracelets.

For Som, who had never done a portrait in his life, the frizzy hair which stood on its end, presented a formidable challenge.

Nearly two hours rolled by - with great difficulty, Som managed to capture a semblance of likeness on his canvas in his initial outline.

No one was quite prepared for what happened next.

The twins Adelita and Ivan had been playing outside with their friend Juanita, who had a chihuahua named 'Aki'. Feeling hungry, the twins and Juanita, accompanied by Aki, decided to head indoors for a bite.

Aki was captivated by Maribel's shiny jewellery and her frizzy hair.

Aki made a beeline for Maribel's hair and her earrings, interposing himself between Maribel and Alonso. Alonso didn't seem to mind this intrusion and began to play with Aki.

Som looked on in horror, realizing that the pose had now changed completely – would he have to start the painting all over from scratch?

Som's fears came true – worse still, Alonso fell in love with Aki and insisted on having Aki included in the portrait, forcing Som to start all over again.

But Aki had no intentions of sitting still and posing for Som. This time, Aki went for the orchids - taking off from Alonso's lap, Aki grabbed two orchids and handed them to Maribel! This of course, got a big Thumbs-up from Alonso, who now put one arm around Maribel and the other around Aki, in a tight embrace.

Poor Som started all over again. But the third time was not to be the charm.

Suddenly, Aki wriggled out of Alonso's embrace and jumped over to Som, sending Som flying and knocking his canvas to the floor.

"Are you okay, Som? Maybe we should leave the portrait for another day when there are no puppies around." cried Maribel.

"I like the puppy in the picture, but agree, he's not going to stay still. Som, can you paint from a photograph? It's not quite the same as posing, but I want a portrait with Maribel and this puppy. I adore this puppy!"

"Of course, Alonso – what an outstanding idea! Paco, please take photos, from as many angles as you can, please. Alonso, I will work from the photos and deliver your portrait to you."

"Fabulous you can finish the portrait after our Mayan excursion. Since we don't have to pose for you tomorrow, how about we all leave tomorrow itself for Chichen Itza and Uxmal? Som, you may bring along Paco and anyone else you wish as your assistants. We leave bright and early tomorrow morning. *Hasta mañana*, Som."

****

When Maribel and Alonso left, an immensely relieved Som hugged and kissed Aki, who had been his Savior. Now, the portrait could be done from photographs and Som could take his time.

Paco asked if Som wanted him to take care of the portrait, but Som declined, "I greatly appreciate your help and advice,

Paco, but outsourcing the entire project to you would be dishonest. That would amount to cheating - I couldn't live with myself if I did that. I will forge ahead with the portrait and let the chips fall where they may!"

Tío Bernardo, who loved any excuse to celebrate, poured everyone a round of tequila, "To Som, an Artist and a Gentleman! To Uxmal and Chichen Itza!"

Chapter 29
Journeying to Chichen Itza!

Bright and early the following morning, Som, Tía Thelma, Tío Bernardo, the twins Adelita and Ivan, Paco, Maribel and Alonso boarded Alonso's private jet for Cancun, *en route* to Chichen Itza. Accompanying them were Maribel's faithful bodyguards, Oscar and Nacho, and Alonso's trusted duo, Juan and Pablo.

Rocky managed to get himself invited to this excursion with one goal in mind - to get to know Maribel and have his tête-à-tête with Alonso.

Not aboard this luxury jet and traveling in coach was poor Dwight - Alonso had indicated to a not so thrilled Dwight that his services would be needed on the Chichen Itza and Uxmal excursions.

This time, Dwight's target would be Barracuda - Dwight's mission would be to monitor Barracuda during the elaborate game that Alonso had devised for the man.

Dwight had vowed to never go near a pyramid again after his Teotihuacan experience, but he did not dare to say no to the Boss.

The evening before the Chichen Itza trip, Barracuda had received an intriguing communication on his cellphone, which read, "I am in receipt of your request for half a million – I invite you to participate in a fun game to double your reward. In this game, you will follow a set of clues. If you complete the game successfully, you shall be awarded a full million! But once you start the game, there is no going back - you must stick with it to the end. If you accept these terms, *'Go to the Mouth of the Well and make your way to the Castle whose steps equal the Days of the Year!'* – your first clue will be waiting there for you."

Barracuda wondered if Alonso was sending him on a wild goose chase. After some reflection, he decided that Alonso would be too much of a gentleman to scam him out of his million – in any case, Barracuda was still in possession of the 'Maribel Kiss' pics and could make them public if Alonso dared to double-cross him.

The prospect of 'doubling his reward' was too much of a temptation for Barracuda to resist. But first, he had to figure out where he was supposed to go to start this game – the clues pointed to some kind of a castle, but which one?

****

In his quest to find the man in the 'Maribel Kiss' pic, Barracuda had spent months, meticulously researching the man's identity and whereabouts. Barracuda had picked up on the fact that this Som was a *learned man,* a librarian working in three libraries, no less. Barracuda's research had indicated that this scholarly librarian was extremely knowledgeable about medicine, science, history and a whole host of other subjects – the man was apparently revered in academic circles as a 'Walking Encyclopedia'.

At Som's 'Dips, Chips and Smoothies' event, Barracuda had cleverly managed to secure Som's telephone number from Tío Bernardo.

Barracuda decided that the scholarly Som would be the right man to solve Alonso's mystery riddle and tell Barracuda where to go.

Barracuda called Som and introduced himself, "Sir, I am a photographer from the UK – I was at your 'Dips, Chips and Smoothies' event and got your number from Tío Bernardo, who told me that you are a man of letters. My dear Sir, I need to solve a series of riddles to qualify for an archeological excursion. I am not much of a historian and wonder if I could pick your brain. My first riddle says to 'Go to the Mouth of the Well and make my way to the Castle whose steps equal the Days of the Year!' – what do you think they are talking about, Sir?"

Som, who had been poring over John Lloyd Stephens' travelogue, knew the answer immediately, "That's easy. 'The Mouth of the Well' refers to Chichen Itza - 'chi' means mouth, 'chen' means well, and 'Itza' refers to the people who lived there. The riddle is speaking of the 'Temple of Kukulcan', also known as 'El Castillo' or 'The Castle' - you see, there are 91 steps on each of its four sides and they add up to 364; the 365th step is the top platform of the 'Temple of Kukulcan', which also corresponds to the number of days in a year! So, you, my dear Sir, need to go to the 'Temple of Kukulcan' in Chichen Itza."

****

Barracuda thanked Som and booked his flight to Cancun for the following morning. Barracuda felt immensely pleased with himself for having gone to Som to decipher this cryptic message, "Alonso thinks he is outsmarting me by giving me silly riddles to solve – true, there is no way I could come up with the answers on my own, but I have this great man, this walking encyclopedia, whom I could call upon. If Alonso bothers me with more of his silly riddles, I will just go to Som for help. I am brilliant!"

It so happened that Barracuda had booked the same early morning flight to Cancun as Dwight. When the two men ran into each other on the plane, Dwight gasped.

"Hello there, I've seen you at Chef Som's 'Dips, Chips and Smoothies' event – aren't you Dwight from El Paso? It's a small world, indeed."

Dwight almost cried out, "And you are Barracuda, the one I am supposed to follow!" but luckily, a tourist with a giant piece of luggage interposed himself between the two men. Dwight was saved in the nick of time from making a major faux pas.

"Ah yes, I remember you – you are Mr. Colt from England, aren't you? Are you off to Cancun for some R&R?"

"I am off to the ruins actually – how about you?"

"Me too – maybe I will bump into you there. Happy travels!" replied Dwight, despondent that Barracuda had figured out Alonso's first clue to start this absurd game.

From Cancun, Alonso and his entourage headed by car to Chichen Itza, as did Dwight and Barracuda.

Chapter 30
An adventure in Chichen Itza!

Some two hours by car from Cancun, lay the magnificent ruins of Chichen Itza, a UNESCO world heritage site. The origins of this Mayan City in Mexico's Yucatan peninsula remain shrouded in mystery, as do the reasons for its abandonment in the 1400s. Over its nearly one-thousand-year history, various peoples left their mark on this city and its monuments, with a fusion of Mayan and other influences.

For each member of Alonso's travel party, the expedition to Chichen Itza signified something special.

For Alonso, it brought back boyhood memories of growing up in the Yucatan – Alonso had climbed many of these pyramids and monuments as a boy and knew them quite intimately.

Som was utterly spellbound by the majesty of these magnificent ruins with their Mayan and Toltec influences – he wanted to visit every nook and cranny described by John Lloyd Stephens in his travelogue, but first, he needed to accomplish an important mission. That mission was to do a series of architectural drawings for Alonso, starting with the 'Temple of Kukulcan' or 'El Castillo' in Chichen Itza.

As climbing of this majestic temple was no longer permitted, Som had a gathering of curious spectators, crowding around him and eagerly watching his every move, as he set up his easel to begin his project.

Som did not mind the presence of Maribel, Tía Thelma, Tío Bernardo and Paco, who were on the team that was rooting for him, but found the piercing stare of Alonso to be rather unsettling.

As the man who had commissioned the artwork, Alonso found himself a comfortable spot to monitor the evolution of Som's drawing.

Rocky was greatly amused to see Som the artist, at work.

Without the benefit of the camera lucida, Som had to resort to using a grid to capture the scale and the correct proportions of this majestic monument. This process took him a while; finally, an outline of the 'Temple of Kukulcan' emerged on Som's Bristol board. For this project, Som had opted for pen and ink, an art medium particularly suitable for architectural drawings.

Alonso was no artist, but even he could tell that the project would take several hours to complete. It would all depend on how fastidious Som chose to be in capturing the details of the monument.

Rocky chuckled, putting in his two cents, "Som, Habibi, your temple seems to be airborne! The Mayans were big on astronomy, looking to the skies for signs from the heavens, but they kept their abodes grounded to the earth. As a builder, I'd say your temple is not tethered to earth!"

"The earth below it shall come later – first, I want to get my temple right."

"Habibi, that's not quite how we build things – we secure the foundation first!"

Maribel quickly stepped in and came to Som's defense, "Let the artist do his work, Rocky! Alonso and I have full faith in our artist. Don't we, Love?"

Alonso agreed that they should all step away and let the artist do his thing. Besides, staring at Som's evolving drawing, stroke by stroke, was getting to be rather monotonous and this gave Alonso a nice way out.

****

Alonso decided to do a walkabout with Maribel and take in the sights. Chichen Itza being one of his favorite haunts during his youth, Alonso knew the ruins intimately and wanted to share his special memories with Maribel.

To Alonso's great surprise, Rocky decided to tag along with the couple!

"Where did this Rocky pop up from out of nowhere? He seems to be excessively pally with Maribel. She is even laughing at his jokes. I don't like it. I should tell Dwight to keep a close eye on this Rocky fellow."

Poor Dwight had the agonizingly boring task of following Barracuda from a distance and sending him riddles at the various 'Rendezvous points' that Alonso had designated for his game. For the life of him, Dwight could not understand why an extremely intelligent and successful man like Alonso would resort to such silly games with riddles, instead of just paying Barracuda off and closing the chapter for good.

Meanwhile, Barracuda followed Som's instructions and made his way to 'El Castillo', the name given by the Spanish to the 'Temple of Kukulcan'. Dwight, who was closely monitoring Barracuda's movements, now dispatched the next riddle to Barracuda's cellphone, which read, "*When day equals night, where does the slithering snake go? You will get your next clue at that spot.*"

Barracuda, who now had access to the librarian who knew it all, simply dialled Som's number. Som answered thinking that it might be Priyanka and was pleasantly surprised to receive another riddle from Barracuda.

Som chuckled, "Ah, you have another riddle for me! I quite enjoy your riddles, my friend. This one is easy – *the day equals the night during the equinox; there are two equinoxes in the year, the vernal equinox in the spring and the autumnal equinox in the fall. On both these days, at sunset, a shadow resembling a 'slithering snake' descends along the steps of the 'Temple of Kukulcan', to meet the head of the serpent at its base. This slithering snake is supposed to represent the serpent deity of Kukulcan.* So, there you have it, my friend, that's your spot!"

Barracuda followed Som's instructions and promptly made his way to the head of the serpent at the base of the 'Temple of Kukulcan'.

Dwight was astounded that Barracuda had figured out Alonso's riddle! Alonso's riddles were Greek and Latin to Dwight – had Alonso not given him detailed instructions as to where these 'Rendezvous points' were supposed to be, Dwight would have never guessed them.

Dwight looked at Barracuda with renewed respect, "This Englishman must be the scholarly type to know all this stuff about a Mayan temple. The Boss must have sensed that Barracuda is a great scholar and designed this elaborate mind game for him. But why would a scholarly gent resort to blackmail? Anyway Barracuda, I am curious to see if you can figure out the next riddle."

****

Barracuda's next riddle read, "*You will find your next clue midway between the Snail and The House of the Dark Writing!*"

Yet again, Barracuda called Som, his human encyclopedia, to get the answer to this riddle.

Som was more than happy to oblige, "*The 'Snail' refers to the building called 'El Caracol' – it has a curved staircase which resembles a snail. 'The House of the Dark Writing' is the one with the mysterious glyphs - it is also known as 'Akab Dzib' and is an ancient pre-Columbian structure, possibly, the oldest in this complex.*"

An elated Barracuda set about in search of '*El Caracol*' and 'The House of the Dark Writing'. Dwight watched his progress, stupefied.

Meanwhile, Alonso returned to the 'basecamp' to check on Som's drawing.

Som had made significant progress, having blocked in the shadows and the lit areas of the temple – now, all he needed to do was to accentuate the 'lights and the darks' and add the final touches to complete his drawing.

Alonso nodded in approval and asked Som if he wanted to take a break.

Som declined, "No, I want to keep going and finish this drawing. If I take a break, the Sun will change its position in the sky and my light and shadow will change drastically. It's best that I finish."

Alonso agreed and called Dwight for updates on Barracuda. Dwight told him that Barracuda was heading towards '*El Caracol*'.

"This guy is pretty bright, Boss! He seems to know exactly where to go – he is always right on the mark."

"Is he? There are a few more riddles to go, so we'll see how he does. Dwight, a new problem has cropped up. I want you to keep an eye on this Rocky fellow. *First, I thought he was after Maribel, but now, I am not so sure. He seems to be after me!* He is following me everywhere. Find out what he is all about. I want a full report."

Dwight sighed, "Poor Boss! If only he could relax and not imagine the worst. But hey, now that Som is no longer his 'Prime Suspect', I guess he is focusing on Rocky. And there may be some truth to what the Boss is saying – this Rocky does seem to be overly interested in Maribel and the Boss. Wonder what his angle is."

To Dwight's utter astonishment, Barracuda made it to the midway point between *'El Caracol'* and 'The House of the Dark Writing'. Dwight duly dispatched the next riddle, which read, "*Go to the 'Bearded Man' for your next clue!*'

Barracuda promptly called Som and asked him who this 'Bearded Man' might be.

Som replied with a laugh, "These riddles are quite clever – you, my friend, need to go to the *'Temple of the Bearded Man'* – *it has a central figure of a man with a carving under his chin that looks like a beard!*"

****

By now, Som was in the final stages of his pen and ink drawing of the 'Temple of Kukulcan' – a crowd of spectators looked on in awe, as Som added his final touches and declared the project as 'done'.

"Paco, Tía Thelma, Tío Bernardo, what do you think? I think I should stop here. If I do any more, I risk losing the likeness I have captured. I am no Frederick Catherwood and I never will be – I hope Alonso will accept the work of this humble artist."

Paco agreed that Som should stop and not overwork his drawing.

Leaving the twins Adelita and Ivan to keep Som company, Paco, Tía Thelma and Tío Bernardo took off in search of Alonso and Maribel, to let them know that Som's '*Obra maestra*' was finished!

No one could have predicted the fate that was to befall Som's 'Temple of Kukulcan' in the next few seconds!

It all happened in a flash, right before Som's eyes.

To Som's utter shock and horror, Adelita and Ivan, each picked up a brush from Som's painting kit, dipped it into the India ink, and sketched in a slithering snake, crawling down the steps of the Temple!

As Alonso, Maribel and Rocky rushed over to see Som's masterpiece, a speechless Som stood there, staring at his drawing which now had two jet black snakes as part of the landscape!

Had it been an oil painting, one could perhaps have touched up the twins' additions and possibly painted over them, but with the India ink that Som was using, there was no going back.

The deed was done!

Tía Thelma apologized profusely for the twins' actions, "We brought the twins here just last year, on the day of the spring equinox - they were utterly fascinated by that shadow, which resembles a slithering snake going down the temple steps! I guess they let their imagination run wild and couldn't resist the urge to add that snake to your drawing. I am truly sorry, Somcito!"

Alonso contemplated Som's work with a twinkle in his eye, "The twins jumped ahead to the day of the equinox and added in the serpents! It is a bold representation - I quite like it!"

"I will do another drawing for you, Alonso! It may not be possible today though, as it is already afternoon. I can do it from a photo or come back tomorrow and give it another shot.' cried Som, still in disbelief that his drawing had been so radically altered in a split second.

"I think it is quite wonderful - it's sort of symbolic and magical! I would like to publish it in my magazine." cried an elated Maribel, who couldn't take her eyes off the drawing.

Alonso chuckled, "Go for it by all means. It's definitely eye-catching! You certainly are a man of many talents, Som. Good show! Now, you must be dying to see these magnificent monuments – Maribel and I got a head start this morning. Don't try to do it all – you can always come back another time."

****

Alonso and Maribel took off to continue their sightseeing, accompanied by their bodyguards.

To Alonso's great annoyance, Rocky joined them yet again! But Alonso had the advantage of knowing every inch of Chichen Itza intimately – making his way towards the 'Nunnery Complex', Alonso cleverly gave Rocky the slip.

Rocky suddenly realized that he was quite alone – he had lost Alonso and Maribel. He made his way back to Alonso's 'basecamp' looking for Som. There, he found Tía Thelma, Tío Bernardo and Paco standing guard by Som's drawing, but Som was gone.

Som finally got his chance to take in the beauty of Chichen Itza. Having spent hours with his drawing which had met a curious fate at the hands of the twins, Som had precious little time left to capture the monuments in this sprawling complex. Som knew he would have to be content with a mini excursion and take lots of photographs – he would be back to enjoy Chichen Itza with his beloved Priyanka.

Som thought of the thrill that John Lloyd Stephens and Frederick Catherwood must have felt, to cast their eyes upon these magnificent monuments which had been mysteriously abandoned around 1400 and reclaimed by the forest. The fanciful names for these structures such as the 'Red House', 'The House of the Bearded Man', 'The Church' and 'The Snail' were coined by the Spanish, who had also given the name 'El Castillo' to the 'Temple of Kukulcan'.

Som began with the very monument that he had rendered on paper, with that added touch by the twins. The 'Temple of Kukulcan' was a remarkable achievement of Mayan astronomy - this Mayan monument also embodied the influence of the Toltecs, who had invaded around 1000 AD, culminating in a merging of the two cultural traditions. The 365 steps in the monument corresponded to the 365 days of the solar year, with the 91 steps on each of the four sides adding up to 364 and the top platform representing the 365th step.

This pinnacle of Mayan astronomy was constructed with such precision that on the days of the spring and autumn equinoxes, the setting sun would cast a shadow reminiscent of a snake, descending the steps to join the stone serpent head at the base of the temple. This snake was thought to represent 'Kukulcan', the serpent deity of the Maya, which was the equivalent of 'Quetzalcoatl', the feathered serpent of the Aztecs.

It was then that Som realized that he was wearing the lucky amulet of Quetzalcoatl that day – the twins had returned it to him the night before. Som thought this lucky charm must indeed be working, as his drawing of this temple was a success. In fact, it was so successful that the twins were tempted to add the 'Slithering Serpent' to it, to 'complete the picture'!

At that moment, Dwight, whose task of the day was to monitor Barracuda and dispatch riddles for Alonso's game, happened to catch sight of Som standing in front of the 'Temple of Kukulcan'.

Dwight gasped, "I went to so much trouble to plant this amulet with a GPS tracker and audio on Som! Then, the kids grabbed it, rendering it worthless for me. Som is wearing my glorious amulet once again, but alas, I am to follow Barracuda and Rocky now."

With limited time on his hands, Som had to be selective - he headed for Chichen Itza's legendary ballcourt, the largest in the Americas. In the ritual ballgame played here in ancient times, a rubber ball had to make it through the stone hoops set high in the walls of the ballcourt – the losers met with the most unfortunate of fates.

****

Meanwhile, Barracuda, with the benefit of Som's sage advice, was riding high. Barracuda made it to the 'House of the Bearded Man' and received his next riddle, which read, *"Look amongst the Skulls of the Departed for your next clue!"*

Barracuda promptly placed a call to Som, "This riddle says something about skulls, which sounds delightfully ghoulish. What do you think?"

Som replied in a somber tone, "Ah, I am afraid it has nothing to do with ghosts and goblins, my friend. The riddle is referring to the 'Platform of Skulls' near the big ballcourt, which was associated with ritual human sacrifice. You can't miss it."

Following Som's directive, Barracuda arrived at the spot and eagerly awaited the next clue. Barracuda felt most indebted to Som – with the help of this gem of a librarian, Barracuda was inching ever so close to his million!

Barracuda's final clue in Chichen Itza read, "Go to the sacred water that quenches the thirst!"

Even Barracuda could guess this one. As he reached the '*Cenote Sagrado*' or the 'Sacred Well', his phone rang again, ushering in his final message for the day, "You have successfully cleared the hurdles of today – this completes the first half of your game. *Tomorrow, go to 'The Tall House built by the Little Dwarf'!*"

Barracuda was overjoyed that he was at the halfway mark in Alonso's game. He called to thank Som, his benefactor, and get a heads-up on the next riddle.

When Barracuda called, Som was staring in awe at the stone hoops in the ballcourt and wondering how those athletes managed to get a heavy rubber ball through them without using their hands, given the stark reality that the penalty for the loser was death.

When Barracuda asked about his final riddle of the day, Som chuckled, "Ah, I see you are moving on to the ruins of

Uxmal. Your riddle is talking of the 'Pyramid of the Magician', the tallest monument in Uxmal, also known as 'The House of the Dwarf' – the legend goes that an enchanted dwarf built it overnight!"

Barracuda thanked Som, "I am immensely grateful for your assistance – I feel I am inching closer to qualifying for my archeological excursion. At least, I am halfway there, thanks to you. I shall make my way to Uxmal now - talk to you tomorrow."

Som smiled, "I too am going to Uxmal tomorrow. Maybe I will run into you there. Keep the riddles coming – I enjoy them greatly."

****

With so little time left before things closed for the day, Som wanted to squeeze in one more monument. He headed for '*El Caracol*', the Mayan lookout to the heavens. This astronomical observatory had a winding staircase reminiscent of a snail. '*El Caracol*', meaning 'The Snail' in Spanish, was carefully aligned with the movements of the Sun and Venus, which held tremendous significance for the Maya.

All in all, it had been an exhilarating day for Som. As the evening drew close, Alonso summoned the members of his expedition to '*Cenote Sagrado*', the last stop of the day.

As there were no rivers in the region, the precious sinkholes were the only sources of water – well-known amongst them was '*Cenote Sagrado*' or the 'Sacred Well', where the Maya propitiated the Rain God 'Chac', whose face was featured prominently in the monuments of Chichen Itza. The sacred offerings to placate 'Chac' included not only jewelry and precious objects, but unfortunately, also humans.

Everyone marveled at the large '*Cenote Sagrado*' and captured it on film. Finally, it was time to leave Chichen Itza, but one member of the Alonso party was missing!

Where was Rocky?

Alonso had been greatly irritated by Rocky's annoying presence all day, but now that Rocky had suddenly disappeared, it was hard to ignore the fact and move on. Alonso asked his bodyguards to look around '*Cenote Sagrado*' and also alerted Dwight.

"Som, your brother-in-law was keeping me and Maribel company for most of the day, but he was not with us in the final leg of our outing. What does he do, this brother-in-law of yours? Could you try calling him? Did he get lost somewhere in the ruins?"

"Alonso, Rocky is a real estate developer. He does own real estate in Mexico – I believe he is quite familiar with the Yucatan. I did try to call, but Rocky is not answering his phone maybe the signal is poor or his battery is low."

A furious search ensued for the missing Rocky.

Chichen Itza was huge and Rocky could be anywhere.

The reality of it was that after losing Alonso and Maribel by the 'Nunnery complex' and being unable to locate Som, a despondent Rocky had set off on his own.

Rocky then found himself going in circles inside a maze of monuments. And so, Rocky simply decided to call it day and head to his hotel in the nearby Valladolid, where he decided to host a surprise reception for Alonso and his party.

About half an hour into the frantic search for the missing Rocky, Alonso got a call, with an invitation from Rocky for a special celebration at his hotel, in the City of Valladolid, about 45 minutes away.

"I had to disappear because I wanted to give you a surprise, Alonso. I had to get away to tell my hotel staff to get things ready for my dear guests. I want to invite everyone for a very special evening!"

Chapter 31
Onward to Uxmal!

It had been a long and exhausting day for all members of Alonso's expedition – Rocky's invitation held immense appeal and was readily accepted.

Imbibing the wonderful cocktails at Rocky's plush hotel put everyone in a jolly mood. The conversation soon turned to the subject of Som, the artist of the day - there was an eclectic mix of verdicts about Som's rendition of the 'Temple of Kukulcan'!

Som thought he had learned a lot from his experience, "My big problem was the Sun – it kept moving and messing up my light and shadow elements. I also got blinded by it. The only way around it would be to draw from photos, which I may end up doing anyway, given the unexpected surprise. But Plein Air painting has its own charm."

Sipping his margarita, Alonso contemplated the man seated across from him, "From what I can see, this Som is a serious artist, laboring over his drawing for hours. His main obsessions in life seem to be his 'Books' and his strange diets. He did not make any untoward overtures towards Maribel today that I could see. Maybe I had him pegged all wrong and Maribel just wants him to write for her magazine and do some cooking demos. But then, there are those pictures of that infamous 'Kiss' that Barracuda has been hounding me with – that kiss makes no sense. The man seated in front of me does not fit the picture. It's all one big mystery!"

Maribel, of course, had only good things to say about Som's drawing.

Tía Thelma and Tío Bernardo apologized yet again, for the twins' surprise contribution to Som's drawing.

Rocky, who had had a head start on the cocktails, was in a great mood, "Som's 'Temple of Kukulcan' looks like one of those medieval castles from a fairy tale – to me, it still looks airborne, as if it were reaching for the Sun. I quite like the added touch by the twins. I might even try building something like it!"

A few margaritas later, Rocky had Alonso's full attention and got down to talking real estate.

Maribel and Som discussed Som's articles for the upcoming issues of Maribel's magazine.

Tía Thelma, Tío Bernardo, Paco and the twins made their way to the swimming pool.

Realizing that Rocky's intentions were strictly business and had nothing to do with Maribel, Alonso quickly warmed up to Rocky and accepted Rocky's invitation to spend the night at his hotel.

****

The following morning, Alonso and company, left Rocky's hotel in Valladolid for the archeological site of Uxmal, some three hours away. Alonso, Maribel, Rocky and their bodyguards were in the first two cars; the third car had Som, Paco, Tía Thelma and the twins, with Tío Bernardo at the wheel.

Suddenly, Alonso felt something whizzing past his car at breakneck speed – the bodyguards of Alonso and Maribel immediately went on high alert, wondering why this driver was overtaking them and positioning himself in front.

Alonso was utterly surprised to note that it was Som's car that had overtaken them. Soon, this car was roaring past all the other vehicles on the highway.

The man behind the wheel of this barreling car, Tío Bernardo, never took his foot off the gas pedal for the entire stretch to Uxmal, winning the admiration of a great many teenagers along the way.

Som once again began to pray that he would make it to Uxmal alive. He knew speeding was par for the course for Tío Bernardo, but with the teenagers egging him on that morning, Tío Bernardo's speeding appeared to have reached a new zenith.

"Where are the cops when you need them? Don't they have cops in this country who ticket dangerous drivers? I wish one would show up immediately and stop this car!" prayed Som.

****

Som's prayers were not answered, but on the bright side, Som reached Uxmal way ahead of Alonso and company.

Dwight and Barracuda, who had spent the night in more humble accommodations, were already there in Uxmal.

Barracuda's first task of the day had been to go to the 'Tall House built by the Little Dwarf'.

As the great Som had already deciphered the riddle for him the day before, a grateful Barracuda followed Som's directions and arrived at the 'Pyramid of the Magician', also called 'The House of the Dwarf', owing to the legend that an enchanted dwarf had built it overnight!

Dwight, who was following the movements of Barracuda, was once again, most astonished, "How does Barracuda know where to go? I think the Boss picked the wrong guy for this stupid game and is going to lose. This guy hasn't missed a single thing so far – I am sure he's going to make it all the way."

Now, Barracuda got his next clue, which read, "Go to the middle of the House of Nuns!"

Wasting no time, Barracuda got on the phone and asked Som to decipher this riddle.

"Ah, I see your game continues, my friend! Well, this one is easy - you need to go to the Nunnery quadrangle, which is made up of four rectangular buildings, in the centre of which lies a courtyard; the middle of this courtyard should be the middle of the House of Nuns!"

As Barracuda set off in high spirits towards the Nunnery Quadrangle, Alonso, Maribel, Rocky and the bodyguards arrived in Uxmal.

Alonso got out of his car and shook Som's hand, "Som, I seem to have seriously underestimated you. I never figured you for a daredevil who breaks every rule of the road! Luckily, there were no cops around. That was quite a stunt you pulled on the highway."

Som was horrified that Alonso would regard him as the perpetrator of this dangerous stunt, "That crazy driving you saw was the doing of Tío Bernardo. Tío Bernardo has apparently been driving like that from the age of seven! There is no stopping that man!"

****

Som set up his easel to start with the day's ambitious project, which was the majestic 'Pyramid of the Magician', the tallest monument in Uxmal and a magnificent example of the 'Puuc' style of Mayan architecture.

The word 'Puuc' was in reference to the hilly region of Yucatan where these monuments were located and also the unique architectural style which flourished there - the face of 'Chac', the Mayan Rain God, could be seen everywhere in the monuments of Uxmal.

Som, as usual, began doing his measurements and using a grid to get the right proportions of this monument. To Som's great relief, Alonso, Maribel and Rocky took off to discuss some potential business ventures.

But the project proved to be quite challenging - the Pyramid of the Magician was built in several phases, with newer structures being added to existing ones over some three centuries. This pyramid also had multiple levels, with a steep staircase entering a doorway representing the mouth of Chac, the God of Rain.

All artists have their good and bad days – Som, who was new to the world of architectural drawing, was stumped by the Pyramid of the Magician!

Som had trouble capturing the *unique shape* of this pyramid with its rounded sides that exhibited a marked slope and seemed to rest on an elliptical base. Also complicating matters for Som, were the ever-changing light and shadows on the pyramid's sloping sides, as the Sun moved across the sky.

Try as he might, the drawing did not work!

Som stepped back and stared at his drawing and back at the Pyramid. He could see its unique architecture, which was unlike anything he had seen, but why was he not able to capture it?

Som's problems were amplified when he heard Rocky's rousing laughter.

"Som, Habibi, this thing you have drawn looks like a lopsided egg that's lying on its side with the top chopped off! There seem to be curious things floating on top of this egg - you had better fix it, or else, Lord Chac, who's up there, might be steamed!"

Rocky's description, unfortunately, was rather accurate.

"I'm stumped by this one, Rocky. Yes, the bottom looks rather like an egg. Alonso, I am going to try something more manageable first, and attempt drawing this pyramid from a photograph."

"Choose whatever pleases you, Som. You are the artist. Come, Rocky – let's leave the poor man alone."

Som was grateful that Alonso and Maribel dragged Rocky away. The worst thing for an artist's morale would be to have someone like Rocky gawking at their artwork and keep up a running commentary that was none too flattering.

With Rocky out of the way, Som set out to find a more manageable monument that would be easier to tackle. Finally, Som decided on one of the monuments of the 'Nunnery Quadrangle' and the 'Governor's Palace'. Som was intrigued by the motifs of the intertwining serpents and the face masks of the Rain God 'Chac', that could be seen everywhere.

These two drawings were successful – Som was relieved that he was no longer 'jinxed'; the unlucky spell of the morning was now behind him.

****

It was past midday when Barracuda called Som with his next riddle, *"Follow the turtles!"*

"Ah, that's easy – the riddle is speaking of the 'House of Turtles' - you should have no trouble finding it."

As a matter of fact, Som himself was headed towards the 'House of Turtles', a delightful little building with a frieze of turtles. Som was tempted to capture it on canvas as it would be an eminently achievable project, but if he did, there would be no time left for anything else.

Barracuda called in with his next clue, *"It's time to follow the pigeons!"*

Som chuckled, "Ah, this one is referring of the 'House of Pigeons' – it should be easy to spot!"

Barracuda trotted over to the 'House of Pigeons' and got his next clue, *"The pigeon flew over to the old woman's house and so must you!"*

Barracuda phoned Som and learned that the 'Old Woman's house' referred to a small complex under a thatched roof, near the Governor's Palace.

As the late afternoon Sun blazed in the sky, an exhausted Barracuda made it to his destination and got his final message, "If you have made it to the 'Old Woman's house', you have succeeded in your quest. You will soon be contacted and the reward will be sent to you."

Barracuda heaved a huge sigh of relief, "I am too old for these games. I am a tired old man wandering about the ruins of Yucatan, following the whims of a crazy man who devised this insane game. But for Som, my angel and Savior, I would have never figured out these strange riddles. I sure hope Alonso will be a gentleman and honor the deal he made. He had better not double-cross me!"

Dwight, who had been busy following Barracuda and dispatching riddles to him, was in utter shock that Barracuda had completed the game! He called Alonso immediately, "Boss, this Barracuda is some kind of a genius! He figured out every one of your riddles and was right on the mark each time. *If you ask me, you should hire the man and get him on your side.* If he can figure out these obscure riddles about the Maya, imagine what an asset he could be to you!"

Alonso was impressed. His respect for Barracuda was heightened, "What Dwight says makes a lot of sense. Barracuda is nimble on his feet and seems to be extremely resourceful – I should get him to work for me. Dwight is good at tailing people, but Barracuda has that *je ne sais quoi* – he is suave and sophisticated. There is an air of elegance and mystery about him… Barracuda would be useful for reconnaissance missions in special situations where Dwight would simply not fit in. Having the two of them working in tandem would be a great idea!"

Chapter 32
Back to Mexico City!

Finally, it was time to leave Uxmal and drive back to Cancun to take Alonso's jet to Mexico City.

Back in Tía Thelma's house in Colonia Reloj, Som started to work on his architectural drawing of that elusive 'Pyramid of the Magician' and the portrait of Alonso, Maribel and Aki, the chihuahua. He also did another version of the 'Temple of Kukulcan' for Alonso.

Upon returning to Mexico City, Dwight was a happy camper. Alonso was extremely pleased with Dwight's services to date, both in Mexico City and in the Yucatan, and had compensated him handsomely.

Even more thrilling for Dwight was the news that Dwight would no longer have to keep tabs on Som – Alonso was finally convinced that Som was not after his Maribel and had taken Dwight off his surveillance duties with respect to Som.

For Dwight, this meant no more waiting around in boring museums, monuments and crowded markets.

Barracuda was utterly astonished when Alonso called, not only offering him the reward money, but also asking him to join his employ, "I was very impressed with your intuitive abilities during that little game in the Yucatan – Dwight told me how you figured out each and every riddle in no time at all. You are quick on your feet and you have the ability to solve abstract problems. I like that in my men! Welcome aboard!"

Barracuda could hardly tell Alonso the truth about how he had solved the riddles by going to Som! The job offer was too good to refuse and Alonso didn't seem to mind that Barracuda wanted to be close to his coffee plantation in Costa Rica.

Finally, the day had come for Som to unveil the grand portrait and the architectural drawings to Alonso. Som stood by nervously, as Alonso stared long and hard at the portrait and the drawings of Uxmal and Chichen Itza.

Finally, Alonso nodded with approval, "I like it! To tell you the truth, I had my doubts that you could pull it off. When I was told that you were this 'Librarian, Chef and Artist' all rolled into one, I thought it was a joke. But Maribel says you are an excellent Chef and the Press loves you. Now, coming to this portrait… I like the way you captured the chihuahua – you have made him the centerpiece of the portrait. I love it! I like the drawings too, especially, the one where the twins added the two serpents. *Felicidades!* You pulled it off."

Som heaved an immense sigh of relief. The portrait project had been most challenging, what with Maribel's frizzy hair, Alonso's tattoos and a chihuahua thrown into the mix. Equally tough had been capturing the rounded sides and the slope of 'The Pyramid of the Magician'. But in the end, it had all worked out somehow - most importantly, Alonso seemed satisfied with the outcome.

Som met with Maribel a few more times to discuss the articles for the magazine.

Rocky, who had achieved his aspirations of getting to know Alonso, now worked towards a higher ambition - meeting Maribel's father, Don Geronimo.

Then, one fine morning, Som got the most wonderful news - Priyanka was done with her assignment in India.

But would Som realize his dream of a romantic holiday with the woman of his dreams? Read on in Book 4 to find out, as the adventures of Som continue on!

About the Author

Venita Jay is an artist and writer with publications in the realm of history of medicine, history, biography, fiction, children's fiction and travel. Her illustrated children's picture books capture the magic of childhood and incorporate the themes of science, nature and geography for the young reader.

THE ADVENTURES OF SOM SHEKAR

Books in this Series:

Book 1 in "**The Adventures of Som Shekar**" delves into an eventful Summer and Fall in the life of Som Shekar, a Toronto librarian and ardent lover of books. In his attempt to lose weight and shape up, Som has an eventful summer. Som's pursuit of a 'healthy lifestyle' brings about several interesting adventures! Som tries many forms of exercise, even taking up Argentine Tango. His quest to adopt a healthy diet causes great annoyance to his family. In September, *the arrival of a new boss turns Som's life upside down!* This strange man has plans to get rid of Som's cherished books! A night of Salsa dancing brings about an unexpected climax! Read on to find out how Som survives this ongoing 'Comedy of Errors' during this fateful Summer and Fall!

Book 2 in "**The Adventures of Som Shekar**" delves into a series of curious prophecies, which manifest in the life of Som Shekar, a Toronto librarian and bibliophile. It all starts with a fortune cookie, which *predicts that Som's life will change forever!* A second prophecy warns that 'aliens' would be landing at Som's doorstep. A strange Winter prophecy *warns that two apparitions from the past would soon manifest in Som's life!* These prophecies come true, turning Som's life upside down, both at home and at work. Read on to find out how Som survives these tumultuous times in his life and this strange confluence of mystical prophecies!

Book 3 in "**The Adventures of Som Shekar**" delves into an eventful Winter in the life of Som Shekar, a Toronto librarian and self-proclaimed chef. When Som decides to take a long overdue vacation in Mexico, strange things begin to happen. *Som meets up with a 'Ghost from the Past' and incurs* *the wrath of a powerful oil baron, who dispatches a detective in pursuit of Som!* Things take a surprising turn, when Som finds himself in the spotlight as a 'Chef'. Som's unexpected foray into the 'world of art' brings about several adventures in Chichen Itza and Uxmal. Following in the footsteps of the detective, read on to find out how Som survives these tumultuous times, weaving his way through the Land of the Maya and the Aztecs!

OTHER BOOKS BY THIS AUTHOR

The Adventures of Little Lee Series:
Little Lee goes to the Moon!
Little Lee goes to Africa!
Little Lee catches a Mystery Thief!
Little Lee and The Lost Island!
Little Lee in California!
Little Lee and The San Andreas Fault!
Little Lee becomes 'Teacher of the Year'!
Little Lee and The Leaning Tower!
Lost in Kusadasi!
Little Lee and The Egyptian Prince!
Little Lee and The Laughing Fountain!
Little Lee goes to Athens!
Little Lee goes to Venice!
Little Lee and The Great Eclipse!
Little Lee and The Bay of Fundy!
Little Lee goes to Agawa Canyon!
Little Lee goes to Santorini!

Other Books:
Mom, You are My Hero!
The day the Sun and the Moon began a conversation!
The Mighty Boar that Saved the Earth!
Mom, I'm hungry!

www.ingramcontent.com/pod-product-compliance
Lightning Source LLC
Chambersburg PA
CBHW031305160726
47993CB00001B/302